Burnt Toast

Burnt Toast

a novel by Peter Gould

Alfred A. Knopf New York 1971

This is a Borzoi Book
Published by Alfred A. Knopf, Inc.
Copyright © 1971 by Peter Gould

ISBN: 0-394-46948-8
Library of Congress Catalog Card Number: 70-147880

Manufactured in the United States of America
First Edition

We consulted the oracle when this book was first begun. This is what came up: "Innocence (The Unexpected)," with one moving line:

"If one does not count on the harvest while plowing,
Nor on the use of the ground while clearing it,
It furthers one to undertake something.
We should do every task for its own sake as time and place demand and not with an eye to the result. Then each task turns out well, and anything we undertake succeeds."

So I wrote this book for my father, and I dedicate it happily to the Farm, to Richard's Famous Spaghetti Sauce, Dale's corn fritters, and the Fen of Wick's wonderful beans; to Marty's potatoes and Fritz's peach wine, Verandah's sourdough oatmeal bread, Ellen's wontons, and Pepper's rice tahini; to Luis his sangría, Lovey's apple crumble, Dougie's vegetable teriyaki, Cliff's miso soup, Raymond's coffee and Bob Payne's popped corn; and to Our Miss Connie's pickles, Stevie D's eggs over (in a covered pan), Cathy's yoghurt, Mad John's lemon pie, Margot and David's stuffed grape leaves, and my mother's chocolate cake, and there's room for more.

Burnt Toast

Part 1

Music, states of happiness, mythology, faces belabored by time, certain twilights and certain places try to tell us something, or have said something we should not have missed, or are about to say something; this imminence of a revelation which does not occur is, perhaps, the aesthetic phenomenon.

—JORGE LUIS BORGES

Maya Maya
All this world is but a play
Be thou the joyful player.

—INCREDIBLE STRING BAND

"Dance till the cookies are done."

—MISS DALE

If you had been walking from the Hollow, up the Old County Road to Captain Packer's place, on a certain twilight in October, you might have stopped at a crest in the road, your attention arrested by a curious apparition in the woods, and a murmur in the air not entirely composed of the wind in the drying leaves, and the rush of a mill stream nearly in spate. You would not have felt frightened, however, for the atmosphere there bespeaks a great peace, almost as if fear were forbidden there and the unbounded emptiness so terrifying in other places were peopled in this place by objects of love and men who are not strangers to each other. Whether or not you knew that each bend and splinter of the road has a name, and that the people who live at the end of the road do not kill animals or work in the city that's not so far away, and that the sign at the crossroads up ahead is the only one in the world that marks the way to Adam's Ear—whether or not you knew these things, I don't think you would have felt afraid to descend from the moonlit road, to take a closer look at what you'd seen.

Come as close as you wish: besides the trees, the water, the rock wall, the hill, and the old family cemetery, half buried in leaves, there is only this to see: a young man has placed a lantern on a slate headstone, and leaned his back against the stone. He's opened a great hand-lettered book, and has just begun to read in a clear and gentle voice. His face is away from the lantern; it's too dark to describe him. But if you sit yourself down on one of the firmer reaches of the wall, or lie in the leaves close by, and have come well-wrapped against the growing chill, you can listen to what he's reading; the story's meant to be passed on. Soon, if his voice turns quieter, you may want to sit closer. Lean against a tombstone too, if you like; nobody he knows is buried here, and even so, the only thing the dead mind is our fear to touch them.

Lie still and listen. You are not the only audience he has.

I found my father fishing on the banks of the moon. He was catching little silverlings on barbless hooks, and throwing them back in. I sat down beside him. I didn't know what to say, or whether he could hear me.

After a while I heard him speak.

Did you write your story yet?

I shook my head. I told him instead about the farm, and the house I built. How I had gathered old beams and planks from downed buildings, how when I lit a fire in the stove the first time, the boards in the walls sighed and stretched, like old men surprised from sleep. How the window looks out on seven miles of hills and meadows to the West, and how the strong wind comes from there, and blows the smoke from my fire across the yard, over the big house and the barn, and through the maple tree gone bare, down across the horse pasture to the old cemetery at the corner of our land.

He didn't answer. I don't think he could. Soon my sister came down the bank with her baby. She dipped him in and he came up silver-covered; she wrapped him in a blanket and carried him laughing back up the bank.

It was time for me to go. I told my father that I would come back, that I'd have the story with me the next time.

I'm on my way to see him now.

My name is Silent and I want to be a poet.

That's what I'm going to be. But first I want to

5

write this story down, about how I found words enough and then some, for all the poems I'll ever need to write, and about how I was granted the meaning of the mystery of burnt toast, and about the vision that gave me the power over all those words. It's a good story, but even if it weren't, I'd write it all down just as I'm going to, because it didn't happen some other way, and because my father said I must write this first, if I want to be a poet. It's one of the three things he asked me to do right before he died. (We didn't know he was going to die just then.) The other two things were these: he told me it was time to begin my quest in earnest, and he asked me, before I left, to widen the second hole in the outhouse.

I mention that just because the outhouse is where my story begins, on the morning of my initiation.

That's where it begins. It ends here, in the evening. I'm not going to tell you exactly where that is, not till much later, but I'll tell you one thing about it. It's an expression we have here:

(To come to this place) you have to pass through Adam's Ear.

The story begins in October. The sun is just coming up over the peach-orchard hill, and my father and I are entering the outhouse. (It's a two-seater.) There's no wind, even in the highest branches of the beech tree. The brown house is behind us, and the barn in front, with the red house attached. The barn has known younger (but surely no more peaceful) days; there's a fading sign to the right of the big door: BY'S FIX-IT SHOP, and we have an old framed photograph in the Green Room of a young man and a woman standing next to the sign—he, leaning against a wooden barrel, holding a spade, and she a broom. She's beautiful, with long earrings, and behind them, deep in the barn, a man with a mustache in a fireman's hat is holding a fly-swat and a snipper. These are the words on the frame of the picture: "Famous Long Ago." Nobody knows who the people are, or why they wrote that on the frame, but it's a nice picture, and it's hanging in the Green Room, right next to the Last Dollar Bill. I think those people must have lived here when the Two were One.

The two dogs and Rosemary the goat have just rounded the wood pile, the old car, and the empty chicken house and are racing up the hill to the peach orchard. That's where they like to shit in the morning. The sunlight has just reached the top of the trees and, even though it's very far away, I can see a few peaches still there. My father can see them too; he has good eyes. He's wearing his red-and-black lumberjack shirt, and green khakis and sneakers. I've got on my mountain boots and overalls, and a red bandana. It's a beautiful morning. It feels like we're going to pick apples.

My father went into the outhouse. As I followed him in, I stepped with all my weight on the threshold, because a good thing always used to happen when I did that. The threshold was just the nearest few feet of one of the great beams that held up the floor of the barn, and it was a little loose at that end. So if you stepped on it hard you could rattle the floorboards in the other end of the barn. It was too far away for you to hear, but the animals right beneath that end could hear, and they always started stamping their feet and snorting. Only they wouldn't do it until a few seconds had passed, because they had to wake up first. They'd start just about as you were turning around, pulling down your pants, and sitting down, all in one motion. Then the hens would hear *them*, and they'd wake up and walk out into the sun. I liked to do that every morning.

We both sat. We were facing the inside of the door, and there were some pretty good pictures there to see. There was old President Eisenhower, Mulla Nasreddin, and Adolf Hitler, and Emmett Grogan, Jayne Mansfield and Pecos Bill. And John Glenn, D. H. Lawrence, Steve Gaskin, Alexander Graham Bell, and Stanley, the explorer. And H. G. Wells, Tracy Nelson, Aleister Crowley, Allen Ginsberg, G. I. Gurdjieff, Robert Burns, and Crazy Horse, Meher Baba, Lawrence of Arabia, Ernie Banks, Catherine the Great, St. Teresa, Ingrid Bergman, Gary Snyder, lots of legs, the Ghent Altarpiece of Jan van Eyck, Mount Shasta, the Marx Brothers, Anais Nin, an angler's map of the Marble Mountain Wilderness, a Triumph 650 chopper, a Springfield Indian, Gregor Mendel, Gaston Bachelard, Mr. Natural, Botticelli's Flora, Nikos Kazantzakis' tombstone ("I want nothing, I fear nothing, I am free."), Anne Hathaway's Cottage, the Blue Mosque, Smokey Robinson and the Miracles, Washington Irving, a painting from a seed packet of a yellow squash called "The Magic Poker," and a photograph of clipper ships loading and unloading in Vancouver harbor, in the very last days of sail.

We didn't talk much at first, my father and I. I looked through the crack into the barn, in time to see my sister, Margot, come in and dig some carrots from the sawdust bin. To her left were crates of old softcover books, and all the maple sugaring equipment, stored until February, and to her right the cleared space where I hoped to build a wood-working shop. There were old stoves piled in the corner. It seemed a shame to throw them away. I looked there for a while, and then I turned around. My father was also looking through a crack in the wall, over on his side. I guessed he was looking at the Suicides' Barn.

That was a good time, for all of us, but you shouldn't think that it was always happy, or that the work we were doing consumed all our attention as the seasons passed us through. (It wasn't meant to; not all of the several worlds are apprehended through action.) There were equal lots of pleasure and pain, which is as it should be; we knew what was important and what wasn't, and sometimes, when I was straining at the cider press, or picking strawberries, or snow-shoeing down to the letterbox after a blizzard, or just sitting up in the orchard at any time of day, watching the farm and the small shapes moving on it, suddenly I'd find myself elsewhere, as far away as anything can be. It's an ocean, but you don't float on the surface (it has no surface); you float somewhere inside it, and you sense other living things floating there too. I've often heard sky pilots talk about it. And whenever I went there I became a star, or a rose, or a silent, glow-ing fish, or a candle bobbing on a raft, or a hollow cir-cle. There was no sound but the sounds that never go away. And sometimes this feeling would fill me as full as an egg fills the shell, and I'd be content, and quiet; other times it would be too much, and I'd try to rush to a place where I wouldn't be hurt if I burst—always afterward that aboutness is there; the wind from the West is always about to blow through me and leave me never to be warm again.

The Suicides' Barn was a place you could go to, on our farm, if you felt like that. It wasn't a bad place; it was a good one. You could go there and see yourself die anytime you wanted to, and then come out and feel what the world would be like if you weren't there. You didn't even have to go all the way inside if you didn't want; you could stand in the doorway, or peer through a hole in the wall. It was up to you, and good to know you were neither the first nor the last to come there. In fact, any time any of us looked through a crack, his back to us, for a long time, or just stared into space as if he were looking through something at nothing, we would say, "He must be looking at the Suicides' Barn."

I don't know whose idea it was to build it; it's no matter—I do know that Memphis Slim once sang a song that went,

> There's no one who's gone over there
> Come back and talked to me about it yet.

Well it was a big empty Irish barn and the hay was always soaking wet and smelling like a draft horse had just passed through. There were heaps of dry sacking that you could lie on and listen to the rain bang on the tin roof, and if a rat popped up in the corner, you could heave a potato at him. There were old shoes and gray clothes and bent birdcages strewn in the hay, and whitewash buckets and broken skis and dusty storm windows. You could lie back on the burlap and look up at the loft and see yourself die. I used to go in there a lot. You could see other deaths there too; anyone who'd ever died in the Suicides' Barn was always dying there, someplace, if you looked. On a typical morning I'd wait in the hay, and soon Marshall would come in with an old vacuum cleaner pipe around his neck. His car was parked in the rear, beside a stream, under a tree. Some hunting dogs would bay. He'd run the hose from the exhaust into the window, and sit in the car and read the morning paper. Perhaps then Verandah would walk in, her long gown like cream; it's the warmest day of mud season and she trudges to where water is rushing warmest, far downhill from the snow, carrying off green aspen buds and dry borage, and she lies down in the mud, opening the veins of her wrists to let the brown torrent take her with it.

Nearby Richard rocks beneath a low eave in his room, tying exquisite knots in a rope that sits in his lap robe, and not too far away Luis slowly smokes a Picayune down to the end. He meets the firing squad again, throwing the blindfold to the ground. And there am I in the high loft—I've seen it a hundred times; it's part of my name—slowly entering a room of the whitest tile. My love walks by me out of the room, water sparkling all over her skin. She touches and kisses me as she goes (down to work on her best drawing, black ink on white stone, called "The Death of Mesmer," in which fine bearded heads without bodies or eyes lie sighing and strewn up the Old County Road). I can smell a peach pie. I haven't carved any wood in a long time, and my hands grow bigger every day as if the work's swelling up inside them. Slowly I undress, step into the shower, and the strong water, perfectly hot, kneads and relaxes my body through. Slowly I turn my face up to the gleaming nozzle and smile. And gently, sublimely, a blue flash leaps from the nozzle to my forehead, and then there's no more to see. It's a peaceful thing, a visit to Death's house before he visits mine. And I can tell he's not going to come for me there or soon, because you'd have to walk clear into the next county to find a tile bathroom, except for the one in Barton's Sunoco Station, and that's gray and doesn't have a shower.

After a while I walk out of the Suicides' Barn (that's a barn we never built; there was talk of building it once, but we decided we didn't have to do it, and there wasn't enough wood). (There were plenty of buildings on our farm that we never got around to building.)

I walk out and go on from there. For a while my self is as Silent as the rest of me always, always, is.

We used to say that man is the only animal that has illusions, and we tried not to have; we tried to be like the others. So when my father was staring through that hole in the wall, I guessed he was looking into the Suicides' Barn. What would you see if you looked there?

Just then I heard a noise outside, of men working well together, and I realized my father was looking at something going on in the yard. I was just about to try to ask him what it was, when he turned to me with his happiest smile (my father was a gleeman) and said,

"How was last night?"

Last night! And my question settled back in me as

the memory of the night returned. I've been sitting here waiting to tell you about it: one of those nights before a great day, when the aboutness is all around, but just on the far side of feeling, like an unyawnable yawn or an unsneezable sneeze. That night, had I swallowed the white crystal or the orange dome, or done the purple dust, or eaten the cactus or the mushroom or the creeper or the fish pill, I would have said it was that process in me that filled me with the cosmic happiness, that there was some heavenly farm of which I was a perfect part, shoveling shit, or liming the great fruit trees in the park, or carving the façade of the great alabaster chicken house. But it was just an October day in the Hardwood; above, the moon was in Libra's second day; that night especially all the parts of the universe seemed to be in purest harmony, as far as I could see, which, all in all, wasn't much farther than my fingers, the farm, the tree-topped Mountain, the road over the Mountain, Spirit Lake, and the bats in the air above.

What happened then won't happen again; it begins the tale of how the burnt toast led to my power vision, and as I look back on it from here, it seems the physical beginning of my quest. It's worth a whole ▬▬▬▬▬▬▬ chapter at least.

▬▬▬▬▬▬▬
The Girl
with the
Butterfly
Between
Her Legs

The night before, for supper, we'd had brown rice and vegetables and sesame toast, and Verandah's onion soup with goat cheese melted in it. Then peach pie and camomile tea. We talked a little about how the day had been and, after our ritual in which each person at the table stands at his place, and the rest of the company cheer and applaud him, I went out to saddle my dapple horse, King Something. I gave him a piece of pie crust. He was glad we were going someplace. My grandmother came out to shake the tablecloth. We watched the crumbs in the sunset.

"Mind you stay away from them Spirit Lake folk," she told me. Spirit Lake's where I was going. I knew she really didn't mind; in fact sometimes I used to think she could remember all the way back to when the Two were One. We had a feud with the Spirit Lake people. The unorthodox said there had never not been a feud, but most of us thought it hadn't always been and wouldn't always be. We had something to look forward to. Anyway they didn't like us stealing their women and we didn't like them stealing ours. But that's the way we did things, and everyone seemed to enjoy it. After we'd brought in a woman, and she'd be hiding her eyes over a teacup and holding her new husband's hand, we could usually hear the Spirit Lake people kicking trees in the Sugarbush, and shouting the four-syllable shout to fill us with fear, and splashing loud rocks in the beaver pond. It was worse in applejack time. But nothing more ever happened, except what you'd expect (women stealing men), and we all did what we had to do. It was a structure; I don't think anyone was ever hurt, not unless he'd made somebody angry.

"Aw, Nana, we're just goin' down to the gas station, aren't we, Silent," my friend Sam explained. He was coming along too.

I nodded. We went over the Mountain. Pipi la Peche, the black puppy, walked with us for a while. We split up at the Forks; she was going the other way. "Don't you run down any deer, Pip," Sam called after her.

Soon we were deep in the woods. We jumped off King Something and he walked off a little way to sit, just past the circle of pines. We sat on a log and watched the sun turn orange through the trees. "Let's have a smoke," Sam said. (He'd brought along some September Gold, the kind we hang in the drying room right next to the sunrise window.) So we passed the pipe between us in silence. It was the best of the year's harvest, except for the part we set aside. We just sat listening to the mill creek tumbling near, and King Something chewing in the kinnikinnic stand. For a few minutes a woodpecker tapped in a tree right above us, and then after he was quiet for a while he started tapping again in a tree that was pretty far away. I forgot it was a woodpecker. It seemed to be a beautiful girl tapping on the glass of her window high in a house. She could see me; I was sitting somewhere between the sun and her red-orange window, and even though I was far away she could tell I wasn't a deer. Her knees and her sleeves were stained with grass, and the back of her dress with moss. She was tapping a song to me:

And where you sit to see the sun come, sun go
I will watch and watch you from my window.

And then she disappeared. I wanted to see her again. Her name was Lila.

There was already something in the air that night. We could both feel it; it wasn't just milkweed or mist, and it grew as we descended the valley that's shaped like a soupbowl, at the bottom of which you come to Spirit Lake. On the far side there was firelight; that was where the houses were, next to the waterfall. There was the great house in the middle, and smaller buildings around it where most of the married people lived, and if you followed the East-West footpath partway up the hill, you came to Fritz's house, which is where Sam was going. Fritz would usually be rocking on his front porch, scratching his teeth and telling some story, drinking home brew (he worked at the sawmill most days, and some days I worked there too), in his big woolen pants with the rope suspenders, tapping his quince-wood cane on the ground, watching the fog form a pillar as it rose from the center of Spirit Lake. There was never a sound there but for owl hoots (no other bird) and deersteps; Spirit Lake's the only lake in the county where the trout don't all leap out of the water, for insects, at sunset. (Sam says that's because they don't eat meat.) Nobody's ever heard a breeze there; the air's so heavy the bats don't even have to flap their wings.

And sometimes you might see an old man come trudging down the path, pulling a skinny mule who's got all the geezer's things tied on his back in a French tablecloth; such old men hang their shotguns on the rusty nails in the trees, then sit on a stump and smoke backy and spit yellow things toward the shore. Some nights after everyone's asleep a leftover catamount walks out on the top of the scree and cries.

I remember one sunset I was standing with Uncle Luis in Fritz's back door; the thick wall of trees was about three feet away from my face. Luis reached down, picked up a sprung mouse trap with a luckless mouse dangling by a tail and a foot, and hurled it far over the trees. This is what he said:

"That's going to land on some golden couple fucking in the woods."

Spirit Lake made you do strange things; it brought forces out from in you that you didn't know were there. You'd have to rub your chin and pretend it wasn't much of a mystery, but if you slept overnight in the woods there, a wild and unreasonable fear, too terrible to name, took hold of you; you'd tremble in your goose-down till you fell asleep, and waken in the morning glad and surprised to see the sun again. We had a feud with the Spirit Lake folk. It wasn't a very big lake. A fox could run around it in a minute.

There's no more to tell about it—water is not my domain—but I want to tell a little more about Sam and me, that night, before he walks up the well-worn path that parallels the stream, past the bachelors' house and the dancing ground to Fritz's place, and I sit and wonder how to find Lila. I don't think Sam's going to come back into this story, after this.

September Gold always made us feel that the falling and dying of a year was good; we learned to see each leaf that fell as a good worker going home to sleep; it was natural that such a cycle would one day carry us with it, away from here. We'd smoke and then creep about in the Hardwood; I'd sneak up on Sam and clap him on the back, and when he'd wheel around, I'd hop up in the air, shout "Ha ha! Ho ho!" and come down as Han Shan, the crazy old monk with matted hair and trousers of leaves and frost on his back, who lived way up on Cold Mountain, purifying his ears. Sometimes Sam would do that to me. It kept us on our toes. We'd often hike into the wilderness to spend a few days fishing; we'd eat parsley and miner's lettuce and cranberries, and drink rose hip and pennyroyal tea. We didn't talk; we ate the pink meat of the Eastern brook trout and watched the fire. (Now fire makes me think of those very fires, and of my father, whom fire consumed.)

Other times we really would go to the gas station; on the way, we'd name all the plants we passed and dream that we were two notorious gun-toting ethnobotanists striding into a Brazilian frontier shanty town. As we came round the church and slowly into the sun-stilled plaza, all the Indians would freeze, and the white men would shiver, and the shoe-shine boys would scatter. Someone would spit and mutter in buccaneer Portugee, "Here comes Silent and his buddy Sam. Better make way." I found out that Sam was an ethnobotanist in a way worth telling: I was meditating one noon in the cactus garden, in the shade of a great Echinocereus. I'd made the mistake of sitting in the path. Sam came walking up the stones; a girl in a plaid skirt was following him. (They were obviously heading for the Amazon rain forest; it was a hot day.) I was humming. I was doing the hum called "Wind-in-the-Cactus-Spines." Sam, his mind in the jungle, crashed right into me, then leaped back about six feet, into the lady's breasts. (She reached her arms around him and tickled his belly.) Then he jumped forward again and hunkered in front of me, sniffing, looking into my face. After supper that night he told everybody about it: "I thought he was a cactus, I swear to God," he said. "Right in the middle of the path."

I have a string of beads around my neck right now.

I carved them myself out of butternut wood. Sometimes I just wear them, and sometimes I sit and pass them across my fingers, one by one. For every bead I could probably tell you a story about Sam, but I think I'll tell only one. I just learned it today. It's called "The Monkey's Revenge."

The Monkey's Revenge

One day, when Sam was feeling a bit under the weather, he went for a walk in the Sugarbush and fell

SAM WALKS UP TO THE SUGARBUSH

in with a monkey who was going his way. They exchanged pleasantries, and then Sam explained that he wasn't feeling very well. The monkey was very sympathetic:

"Easily remedied," the monkey said, "you just have to show your body who's the master." Then he showed Sam a dance he could do to drive out the sickness. Soon Sam was feeling as fit as could be.

"Monkey," he said, "why don't you come and have supper with us tonight?"

At supper that night the monkey ate all the banana bread and pissed all over the corn fritters. Sourdough was the first to complain:

"This has gone far enough, Sam," he decided. "Last month it was a raccoon that pelted us all with the stuffed mushrooms, and now this. You'd better get that monkey out of here." Some of the other people agreed.

Sam walked the monkey back up to the Sugarbush. I watched them through the window. The monkey was holding Sam's hand; you could tell that they were both very hurt.

Sam tried to apologize.

"That's all right, friend," the monkey said. "Some people find it hard to accept a person for what he is."

They parted with a brotherly hug, and then Sam started back downhill, mulling over the wise thing the monkey had said. Then he thought of something he wanted to ask the monkey, and he ran back to where he'd left him. The monkey was sitting under a tree, his chin in his hands.

"Stand back!" he shouted. "Stay right where you are."

Sam stood still.

"Drop your pants!" the monkey commanded.

Sam dropped his pants. He didn't have to be told things twice. The monkey hopped up and down laughing, and pointed at Sam's pecker shriveling up with fear.

"Why are you doing this?" Sam asked him.

The monkey explained. "I'm a monkey; I'll never be anything but." Then he raced around Sam, three times counter-clockwise, and three clockwise, chanting an evil mantra. When he was finished he started over the hill. When he was almost out of sight he stopped for a moment.

"I'm going away now," he said. "You'd better not move."

"For how long?" Sam wanted to know.

"Till the apricots ripen on that tree," the monkey said, and then he was gone.

So Sam stood there for a long, long while, lamenting his misfortune. He hoped nobody would come along and see him. The first time he glanced up at the tree to see if it was time to move yet, he got quite a surprise.

"It's a fir tree!" he exclaimed. "I could stand here till my beard tickles my tool, and the apricots would never ripen there." So he pulled up his pants and started down out of the Sugarbush. When he came out of the woods he found that the hill was covered with snow, and where the farmhouse had been at the bottom, there was a wind-swept lake with a tremendous rock rising from the middle. There was a telephone on top of the rock. It was ringing. "Better answer that phone," Sam thought, and he slogged the quarter mile through hip-deep snow, dived into the lake, wrestled six crocodiles on the way across, and scrambled and tore up the sheer rock face, falling back many times into the water. Finally he made it to the top, and picked up the phone.

"Hello!" he bellowed.

"Monkey here," said the voice.

Sam gave him a piece of his mind. "You'd better put the farmhouse back," he told him, "just as it was. We've had enough of your tricks!"

"All right," said the monkey. "Don't get excited. I didn't mean you any harm." Sam heard him call out to one of his wicked assistants. Instantly the rock turned back into the farmhouse, and the lake and the snow disappeared. But Sam found himself stuck in the chimney, with the telephone in his lap. You should have heard him holler.

Pepper came running into the kitchen. "What's all the commotion about?" she asked.

"I answered the phone," Sam explained, "and now I'm stuck in the chimney."

"The phone didn't ring," she told him, "I would have heard it if it had. I was sitting right next to the kitchen."

My father turned to me. "Phone hasn't been hooked up for years, has it, Silent?" I shrugged. I didn't know we had a phone.

My grandmother crouched in the fireplace. She was trying to poke Sam down with a broom. "You'd better come down out of there," she warned, "you've got a lot of explaining to do."

We had to take the chimney apart. It was time to build a new one anyway. We scraped the soot off one of the bricks and this is what it said:

"This chimney will be destroyed to liberate a man named Sam. No blame."

We all gathered around Sam. "Do you feel like telling the people what this is all about?" Sourdough asked. Sam tried to explain, but the words just wouldn't come. So we let it pass. No one was ever forced to speak, and we were happy to have Sam out of the chimney. I built a fire in the campfire, and Sam and I sat there thinking on the stumps, almost until the sun came up. Once, about midnight, he raised his head as if he thought I was waiting for him to tell me, but I stopped him; I waved both my hands over my head, as if I was shaking the dust from a long, long blanket, and said, "That's okay. That's okay." That was a gesture I'd learned from him.

That's the story of the day we took the old chimney down, and nailed the telephone to the wall in the Green Room, right next to the portrait of the last kingfisher, that my father painted ("From real life," he said). We never mentioned it again, until about three years later, when a colorful plastic postcard arrived in the mail from the islands. It was a picture of a naked black maiden, with a monkey in a loud shirt sitting on one of her thighs and holding her nipple. There was no mistaking who the monkey was. He'd obviously come a long way. This is what the postcard said:

"Dear Sam, /Greetings from the Tropics /where life is cheap. /With fond memories of /our days in the Sugarbush /together. Your old friend, /The Monkey."

Ray brought up the subject at dinner. He washed down some turnips and said,

"That postcard you got from the islands today: is that the same monkey who came to dinner the night you got stuck in the chimney?"

Sam said it was. The very same.

"I sometimes think about him," Ray said. "We weren't really very kind to him."

"He was cute," Kathy said. She had a faraway look in her eyes.

"I guess it was my fault," said Sourdough. "I reacted out of proportion."

My grandmother had something to offer: "If he ever comes this way again, I'll see to it that he feels right at home. Like one of the family."

"If you do that," Sam said, "I'll carry him out of here by the tail and throw him in the Beaver Pond."

There was a stunned silence around the table. Finally my father spoke up. "I'm really flabbergasted, Sam. You and the monkey were such good friends."

"Nothing clings!" Sam roared. He seemed pretty angry. Luis put down his glass; there was more to this than met the eye.

"Don't shout at the table," my grandmother scolded. "We're just talking about a harmless little monkey."

"That's easy for you to say," said Luis, "you didn't get stuck in the chimney."

Everyone took that for what it was worth. It's still one of our favorite expressions.

Sam's gone away, and I didn't find out the true story until today. Before he left he gave me a letter to carry around in my pouch. "Open this and read it," he said, "if you ever see a monkey in the Sugarbush."

When I folded it up again I noticed this postscript on the back: "If you get stuck in the chimney, that's okay. That's okay. Just tell this story and then go on to something else."

24

Sam and I were pretty good friends. Sometimes we'd go to the gas station and kid around with the town people there. They'd complain about how many Saracens were moving into the neighborhood. Soon men from Spirit Lake, and later men from the Baby Farm, would come, and there'd be some good talking and listening then. I'd usually sit a few feet away; I'd lean back against a gas pump and eat some ice cream or some nuts and watch the others grouped before the plate glass window. But the times I liked best were the times we'd just sit, Sam and I, and each think about his own power vision. I don't know exactly what his was because we didn't discuss it—you shouldn't tell your vision before you have power over it, but I think it had the lips of a beautiful girl in it, and a clear stone, a baseball park, and a hobo disguised as a brown bear. Those were the things I caught a glimpse of. I think he knew a little bit about my burnt toast, because I sometimes heard him whistling a bar from one of my songs about it.

After the visions had gone, we'd talk about whatever there was: the tractor, the barn, a trout, a Syrian salad, fried corn pone, a birch tree—I always liked talking with him; you could tell he was content to be inside his own skin. Once he had sat himself down in the warm grass, and his roots pushed through and spread down deep into the ground, Bigfoot herself couldn't budge him. ("I'm eating," he'd say, "don't move me, Girl.") So when we talked I knew he wasn't about to vanish if I took a long time thinking between words, and I always did. He wouldn't even finger a mushroom or pick his ear. Most people didn't know how to listen; I couldn't even start to talk before I felt as if I were lying on the hard ground, with the man or woman sitting on my chest, yawning, scratching, farting, dreaming, wondering why I hadn't spoken. A word would slowly bubble up from my word-hoard, like air through honey: I'd grab hold of it while it was still in my mouth, and think about many different things, all at once: Do I really want to speak? Is this the word I want to say? Is it the truth? Have I ever said this word before? Was it difficult to say it then? Why do people have to talk? Why do I think things like this? Do other people think like this? Are there other people? What makes me speak? What makes me Silent? To whom am I speaking? Do I know him? Who am I? All these questions came and went in a few seconds, and then the word would come out of my mouth, or not; if not, some other word came soon, similarly distilled, or none at all. So it went. But it wasn't that way always (and it's not that way any more); that's not how it was when I ate the cactus, or smoked September Gold, or talked with Sam, or with a few other people whom I trusted, or with my father, or with the animals, or with a girl I was making love with, or slowly coming about to love. It was important to me to have those times, because in order to understand and gain power over words, I first had to accept the hard times as a part of me—not, that is, as visited upon me, and not as the whole of me, either.

I didn't know where to begin. In fact, I hadn't even thought of beginning, yet. The call always comes from some place else; it comes to remind you of a mystery you're born with, as people in old times used to be born with Sin (so I've heard). That night on the near shore of Spirit Lake, I wasn't thinking about finding anything out, except perhaps what Lila smelled like, when she was close, and how she moved. I was only dimly aware that the vision of burnt toast that I had barely had, a few times, and was beginning to have again, that night, was, in all its various disguises, a nameless ascendant mystery to me and for my good, a game and a code in my blood, stirred to awakening by my dreams, by Spirit Lake, by Sam and Lila, by my father about to vanish without ever going on his quest or sharing mine, by my lungs filled by fresh air or the sweet smoke, by the forest, the moon, the white birch, the cottontail deer, by anything I see as if for the first time, and by the space in my mind that's filled and filling with memory, even as I write this. So I just sit, very still, on a log beside the shore, as red-bearded Sufi Sam leaves to walk west to Fritz's place. He gives me a big friendly hug as he goes—he seems to know what's about to begin, seems to know (with both regret and joy), as well as I do now, that he's not going to appear again in this book, and he slowly makes his way around the lake, stops at the waterfall on the other side, where he knows I can still see him, and waves once, a long one, before he disappears into the brush.

The Girl
with the
Butterfly

For a long time I just sat on that log, as the darkness grew complete. I didn't feel like moving. Whatever was going to happen could happen there. Back up on the ridge, where the Spirit Lake spur comes off the main trail, I could hear King Something, chewing still. There was some really sweet grass up there, that always came up late in the year, because that bend in the trail was the last place in the Hardwood to lose its snow in summer. (You could feel the cool on your face when you were still half a mile away.) King Something never climbed down the spur—we had an understanding—he always stayed up there chewing, right beside the big old juniper where there used to be a sign that said: SPIRIT LAKE $\rightarrow \frac{1}{4}$ mi.

The bats had gone away, and the column of mist, too. In their place the moon came, and with it a sil-ver-blue dust seemed to cover everything in sight. We had quiet on the Mountain, but it wasn't like the quiet I heard that night. More than nothing stirred the surface of the lake; something was consciously not-stirring it, I thought, bound between the firelight on the far shore and the glowing worms on the near. When I shut my eyes I saw the same things; every-where that I could feel there was no form yet but the promise of form, and I reached my hand up to pluck the last fresh inches of a spruce twig, peeled off the outer bark and sucked the inner, while I waited. It has one taste in summer, and another in the fall.

Across the lake, I could see one of the unmarried men carry a flaming brand from the kitchen house to light the fire in the dancing-ground. When the fire rose I saw that most of the Lake People were mus-tered in a circle round the ground, and four masked figures were walking from the great house to the fire. They were dressed in wide, striped pantaloons, with Paisley sashes and colored vests, bells on their ankles and glowing paint on their arms, fine hair to the waist and full beards, with masks serenely blue, on which

28

the eyes were painted sleeping. I recognized the four: they were the journeymen musicians who came our way every autumn in disguise, to give us the newest music. (Nobody knew where they got it from.) I was happy to see them at Spirit Lake; I knew they'd be up at the Mountain tomorrow, and it would be a feast day. We always said the leaves themselves waited to turn their brightest until the day the four musicians came.

Six women, my father's sister among them, brought a woolen rug they'd woven for the players to sit on. There was a long silence then; the four just watched the fire while their instruments—a drone, a drum, a pipe, and a dulcimer—seemed to hang in the air before them. My moon shadow moved far down the log, before the first note floated across the lake to my ear.

I wish you'd been there. I've no way to make the sound for you; nor should you strain to catch more than the idea of it. This much I can tell you: in those days rare new sounds were just coming into the popular music of the Hardwood. People said it was the influence, come upland and upriver, of the island music in the sea far to the south, where many people from the East had come to help harvest fruit and cane. Other people said that the music had come down from the forests of the North, which the Downeasters had long since left to the immigrant Himalayan loggers, who liked it there. I believe a third story (I made it up myself): that the music was taught, for some purpose, to these very four musicians who came around each autumn, by world-traveling dolphins, and it had to do with the sound of heartbeats and breathing, heard under water, and the cries they send out to find their way (relative to each other, not to the ocean) through the vast swells, and the silent forests of seaweed that stand around them. But how or why the dolphins came to teach their music, or the musicians to learn it, I don't know.

I saw the glass rings on their hands sparkle as they started to play, and the eyes on the circle of faces slowly close. Behind their heads I thought I saw the high yellow grass give way as the forest animals came forth to listen. Slowly in time with the drone the smallest wave took form on the far shore, and moved over the water to ripple at my feet. In its wake came a single dulcimer note—I saw it coming before I heard it, a glowing sphere of swamp fire that seemed drawn to me. It floated up to my forehead, touched me between the eyes like a fox's tail and dissolved, shaking my whole body, once and then the echo, as if a hand had plucked my spine. When the next note arrived, my eyes were closed.

I don't know how long I listened there, nor how lingeringly note followed note. When I looked again, the fire hissed low and dancers whirled around it, on purpose to go mad. A wind that resembled a gander filled the skirt of one girl, and she cast a wild glance in my direction, fled away from the circle like a butterfly, and plunged into the woods near the shore. The four musicians had all risen; they seemed at once to be spinning and standing immobile, their many arms frozen in gesture, their world-blind masks turned toward me. Animals of the farm and of the Hardwood had gathered at their feet. Suddenly the shaman, Leo the frail man-woman Catalán, leaped through the fire to dance the Death of the Serpent, and as he danced he moaned (I don't remember it all): "Silent! I am old, I know nothing. Ahh, the unseizable totality! The moon! The red room! The girl! The pomegranate! Ahh, the deerness of the deer!" When the last word fell from his lips, he bent to the ground like a broken dandelion, and lay flat, continuing his dance with his fingers and wrists.

My eyes pressed shut again, hands covered ears, as if to trap his words inside my mind. But they wouldn't lie still; they rushed all around within. So I hummed. I did the hum called "Trout-Sleeps-in-Ice" till the words and the dancer came to rest inside me, ikons forever: "Silent! The girl! Ahh! The deerness of the deer!"

Many more things I had to tell you about that night, but I'm going to save most of them for some other time, or not tell them at all. When you have so many words, some of them are just bound to be lies. If, while those four musicians played and the shaman danced, you found yourself thinking, "Something has changed; this can no longer be true," you were probably right. But that's not important; what is important is that in making that statement you have now come to stand at a critical place yourself, withholding what you can, looking to see who's watching you, pausing again on the road, arrested by this light in the forest; or hesitant at the crossroad that could bring you to Adam's Ear; or electing to wait for me, as King Something always does, at the top of the trail to Spirit Lake. What will you do? What is about to happen? Will you still be here when it's through?

It's just a reflex, something we all do. In such a

way I wait to join my father, though I loved him. Just to indulge the desire we feel, for the orderly transference of power, when the void before and behind all words looms into view; dualities ("me" and "you") and all provisional symbols go away, and we have a chance to contemplate "Being in relation to itself, and not in relation to oneself." (I read that in a book.) From this contemplation my power vision is to come, since all things come from that; it has no beginning or end, and words do very little more than begin and end.

Unseizable, and we go on trying to seize; the same, and we apportion names. But look: the wise man dances free from himself and cries, "Ahh! The deerness of the deer!" Here is what words are composed of (words break down): eternity, mind, fire, and wind, and each word tells as much as a musical note, a tombstone (what is it for?), a wall around nothing, a path in the ocean; the smell, in the middle of the great Hardwood, of a lone tree trunk where a dog paused long ago as he passed through.

I've paused, too, to tell you things you already know: that all wells are filled with water, that all dead men are present in this graveyard, that we are about to behold the burnt toast (that's just a name I have for it), and that, in any sense that finally matters, nothing that happened at Spirit Lake was real—though happen it did; I was there.

W hen I stopped humming, the fire had gone out. The moon was behind the trees. I couldn't see much, so I closed my eyes again. I guessed that the dancers, the shaman, and the four musicians had formed the closing circle and sat now listening to the quiet. There were some sounds in it, some too far away to hear:

Behind them on the hill Fritz's rocking chair creaks and he laughs once in the darkness. Annie and Pony have come to visit. Annie's leaning her thighs on the railing and holding Pony in her arms. Sam's inside the house (you can't see him), throwing some wood in the stove. When he opens it up, some light comes out the window and Fritz can see Annie's face. Then the stove clangs shut. Sam's whistling. He's whistling "The Big Rock Candy Mountains." He's just come to the part that goes:

> *O I'm bound to go where there ain't no snow*
> *And the rain don't fall, the wind don't blow,*
> *In the Big Rock Candy Mountains.*

A mile away, over the Mountain, my father quietly closes the door of the house. He's outside. Pipi just makes it through following him before the door is completely closed. My father looks around and listens. He wishes he hadn't awakened. He walks out to the garden; it's in the meadow on the far side of the tractor shed. It's got a fence of weeds. He sits down on the ground, pulls up a late white radish and wipes it with what he's wearing. Then he takes a big bite out of it.

Up on the ridge King Something snorts. He's discovered a small patch of wintergreen a few steps to the left, and has just put his mouth over the first red berry.

Beside the lake, the girl who left the dancing-ground has come halfway around to me. She's walking as fast as she can, but not as fast as a fox. Sometimes she bends to pick twigs out of her toes. It's very dark. Where she has just stepped, on a slope, a few pebbles roll into the water.

I don't remember any of those sounds. Something else was happening to me. It didn't take very long. When it was all over, Sam was still whistling. This time he was whistling:

> *Where did you come from*
> *Where did you go*
> *Where did you come from*
> *My Cotton-Eyed Joe.*

My father was still chewing that radish. His eyes were wet. Pipi had come up and sat down in front of him. All the wintergreen was gone, the roots too, and King Something moved back to the grass. The girl had stepped from the trees into the clearing and sat beside me on the log. She put her head beside my neck. She put her arm around my back, and then I put mine around hers. Her breath came into my ear.

This is what happened to me in that time:

I seemed to awaken, although I hadn't slept. I was in a red room. All the walls were red velvet. The room was at my back; I was looking out the window. The window was shaped like a slice of bread. There were flowers on the sill. Their stems were made of pipe cleaners and their heads were cut-glass spheres, purple, red, orange, and yellow. They broke up the sunlight, and some of it fell on my hands.

There's a wide bright river outside, verged by a levee as far as I can see each way, with people on it who come and go. Beyond them the sails of pleasure boats, and one skiff slowly rowing past, nearly tipping its passengers into the river: four fishermen, rowing; a robed man holding a lantern; and a cat. They're all bent over the water, looking for a certain fish. The people on the boardwalk drift to the sides, making an aisle among them. Then seven horsemen gallop past, whips rising and falling on their mounts' steaming sides. They seem to be traveling very fast, but they actually pass by slowly, and each rider pauses once, his wrist and whip behind his head, to turn his face up to me at the window. When they're gone the boardwalk is as before. An Austrian flower vendor walks up to each couple and sings, "Are these your flowers /Whose flowers are these?" He has a companion who's playing a concertina. They stop in front of my building and someone in a window above me throws them a guilder.

Across the way the boardwalk widens into a little square that juts over the water. There two children, a boy and a girl, or a girl and a boy, are sitting on a statue of a turtle, playing an interesting game. First he says "Hey," and then she says "Hey what?" and he says "That's what." Then they play another game. She says "Do you know what?" and he asks "What?" and she answers "That's what." Their governess is sitting on a bench with some other governesses. They're all eating chili pie.

Then I saw myself walk onto that square, between the turtle and the bench. I'm wearing a bowler hat, and a pink crepe shirt with billowing sleeves. The children call me a name as I walk past. I climb a wooden staircase down to the pier that floats far out on the water. At the end of the pier people have formed a queue. A great riverboat's pulling alongside. I wait with the rest as the gangplank swings down. The steamer has come across the great water. There are two versions to what happens next:

My love comes down the gangplank. She's had such a sunny crossing, catching the spray in the bow, that her hair has turned nearly red. She's wearing an emerald dress with roses on it, and it comes to the middle of her thighs. She opens her bag for the customs inspector as her eyes search the crowd for me.

Or: My love comes down the gangplank. The weather's been wet, and she's spent most of the voyage inside. She's wearing pink dungarees gone white at the crotch, and my blue Italian undershirt, sleeveless. You can see her brown nipples through the shirt. She doesn't have any luggage. The customs inspector puts his tongue into her mouth as her eyes search the crowd for me.

We're happy as can be, hugging and walking back along the pier, up the stairway, between the bench and the turtle, across the boardwalk, and out of my view. Now I turn from the window and she's there, lying on the brass bed. If I remember nothing else, I will remember how she climbed up the stairs two at a time. All afternoon we make love; even when we lie still she continues to rock slowly, as if she's a ship. Sunset comes, the room deeper red; I rise to put a coin in the flame heater and turn it up, and stand at the window again. Most of the people have gone from the boardwalk. The horsemen go by again; they're riding in the same direction. A man steps out of a restaurant below to toss a Greek salad. He catches it in a wooden bowl as it floats down.

The shriek behind me. I whirl about to see her leap back from the heater, skin aglow, hands beating at her burning hair. For just a second I watch her dance (fire commands a profound attention, that wells up on its own), then run to throw a blanket on her head. We lie together a long while, her face hid in my neck, my fingers combing hair from her hair. That's how we fall asleep. A long time later I wake from a dream, to pull the covers closer round us. I look around in the dark. The red room is gone. There's not a ripple on the lake; you can see faint stars there. The only sound is the breathing of the girl on the log beside me, and a rub of bark as our bodies settle to each other's shape, slowly and with untellable release, as when two bodies of water finally touch, when the last bit of soil between them has washed away.

She breathed a long time, mouth to my ear, so long I forgot she was there. I forgot a girl was there. I thought I'd put my arm around a field of wheat.

Each time she breathed I heard the sound a year makes as it passes through a field of wheat. When she took some air in, that was spring, and then the seeds lay in her lungs a while, came through the surfaces in summer, and after the body harvested them, took the harvest away to be food, the wind came again, from in her, to blow the chaff out of her lips on the air. So the years passed, and from year to year I was nothing but the knower of this.

And then the wheat was gone, but the wind stayed

on. It didn't hum a cycle any more, but just the one sound, "Wind-Searches-for-Wheat." Up hill and down; the mud itself turned yellow to please it, and soon the wind was still. Then all that remained was a yellow source of light, with some red behind it, and it seemed at once so simple and so beautiful to me that I wanted to show it to the girl beside me, and I tried.

How could I try something like that? I couldn't be more alive than I was. It might happen to her, as it happened to me, but I couldn't wish for more. So I tried to drive the wish from my mind, tried to listen and not to think. And when I did that it was not long before the yellow light revealed itself as a surface and I caught a glimpse of the dark behind it; I realized I was sitting on a surface, on an edge I could not leave except to fall from it, and fearing to move or speak, I thought the question "Lila, are you here?"

That's when I heard a third sound. I heard her laugh. I turned to look at her. It was a laugh not much bigger than a smile; it went a few feet, and then it fell into the lake.

I decided to say something to her. This is what I said:

"Do you remember how we met?"

It's not that I don't have a good memory. It gets by. If I had to I could probably remember all of the versions of the story of how we met. I just like to hear her tell it, because she makes it into a good story, and embroiders it differently every time. (It's not that she doesn't have a good memory.) Whenever she changes

it, she has a good reason. "New beginning: new end,"
she says and smiles.

   I'm listening, too. Remember, if you can, it's just a
story.

   (You know the truth yourself. I hadn't even met
her yet.)

How
We Met
(by Lila)

Silent, I suck my tooth when I think how it all
might not have happened as it did. You might still be
troubled in mind, and I might still be wandering on
the great mountain that gives this land its name, past
hope of ever finding you.

   Because that's how it began. You were young, but
you had done everything you could possibly do. Eaten
mushrooms in dankest Guatemala, hawked yoghurt
and pocketwatches in the Old Bazaar in Stamboul,
wrestled octopi in the Bay of Biscay, sunbathed and
loved your first love on Half-Moon Beach while the
mortars thudded just over the farthest palms. Finally
put ashore here in dead of night, you worked your
way up in the ranks, ingenuous. Mighty men breathed
in your face. You carved the altarpiece in the chapel
of the King himself, and secretly taught the Dauphin
all you knew, of the world and what's in it. There was
talk of a trail of spurned women, sick with desire,
thighs wrapped about fragrant pillows, lonely in their
chambers.

   (When she said that I could scarcely sit still.)

   What did you have on your mind?

   You left the keep of the King, and you wandered

39

around, from town to town, disguised as a lame tool-and-die man. Civil unrest was abroad in the land; there was little respect for law and order. The air and the water and the trees, the fish that swim, and the birds that fly cried out for release, and when the inevitable battle came you fought long and well on the right side. Your reward was the reward of us all.

You longed for home. So you set off East, to the forest and the farm. Everywhere you traveled the old and the young were at peace. Natural abundance grew over the land. It was said that a virgin with a sack of gold could ride unmolested from one coast to the other.

You came to where the Southern Highway meets the Western Highway, and there you sat down on a salt lick to see what you could see. There was a speck on the way coming North, and as it grew in your direction, you made out a person a-horseback, and you brimmed with wonder.

Do you know who it was?

("Who?")

A virgin with a sack of gold.

When she came abreast of you, you leaped from the salt lick, spilled the sack to the ground, flung her on top of it, and made love to her so many times that the gold ran freely with her maidenly blood. You had never believed what they said, and neither had I.

Once again it was very quiet. I heard King Something take four hesitating steps down the trail, wondering if he ought to come after me. From up on the ridge he could see that the moon didn't have far to go, and we'd better think about going to sleep. Lila stood from the log, turned to face me, then sat on my lap with her belly against mine and her arms around my neck, my forehead upon her lips, my chin just above her breasts. (It's our favorite position. Scarcely could the two aspects of the revealed Absolute be represented in a more majestically intimate way.)

"What happened after that?" I asked her.

She didn't answer. She pursed her lips, right there on my head, trying to remember.

"Did people come by?"

"People came by," she said, "yes, many people. They weren't afraid to become involved. If they came from the West they paused to ask if you needed any help, and you told them no, everything was under control. If they came from the South they asked me if I was in trouble, and I told them no and showed them how tight I was holding you. It was nice of them to ask. We stayed as we were till sunrise. Then we went away from there. We came here."

"What are we going to do here?" (I thought she might know.)

"You'll be going home soon, after one more thing has happened. (Maybe two.) Tomorrow is your initiation, and the first day of your quest for words. I am meant to help you on your quest."

She really did know! I was so excited I bounced her up and down with my legs. In each of my hands I squeezed half of her beautiful ass. Things have a way of working out. I wondered what was in store for me next.

I leaned my head to the right to put a kiss on her neck. My eyes took in the darkness where the lake was, behind her. Then suddenly my mouth froze in motion and fell, my eyes went wide, my body trembled once, head to toe, and I squeezed her so hard she cried out in surprise. Not an arm's length from where we embraced, seeming to float in the air, with a sharpness of outline and a complexity of inner form it had never possessed before, the vision I had seen at my awakening here, and had glimpsed but rare and dark suggestions of, ever since:

Burnt Toast.

I may as well tell you now: you've set off on the wrong foot already, if you've just happened to code, somewhere into your memory, a slice of white toast, mildly scorched, even blackened, buttered or no, hanging in the air over Spirit Lake (the image of fire over water). That's not what I saw; that's just a name I have for it. Though it presented itself as a piece of burnt toast, it seemed to say, in the same instant, this is only a symbol: what I am like is what I am not; things that you see are as provisional as words themselves, temporary perceptions that last till you know what's really there. So as soon as I saw the burnt toast suspended there, my vision of it was already beginning to change—surface dissolving, new surface behind—though the first appearance remained in the form of its name. Only now (having come here) do I know that all the visions and hallucinations you have, till the eternal one fills and so closes your eyes, are nothing but further information about the vision you saw, the very first time you opened them to the touch of the dim red light in your skull, and a strange earthly reality took the place of the first, silent one.

The burnt toast changed. (What it meant is changeless.) These are some other things I saw, and did not see:

Summertime. My mother has not awakened to give me breakfast. I go out to the strawberries. I look at the ground and the vines and the berries through cupped hands. The sun rises in the dew.

There's only one lamb chop for my grandfather and me. He takes the bone, and gives me the meat in the middle.

We're playing a game. They hide an object somewhere on the farm, then come and say what it is. The children search for it. When you find it you have to holler its name, and the name of the place where it is. I'm the first to find it. It's a red plastic purse, flat on the bottom and round at the top. I open my mouth to cry the victory. Nothing comes out. I stare at the purse for a while. Then I pretend I didn't see it.

Our dog wounds a rabbit. The rabbit gets away. Their tracks in the snow.

A dream. My father has died. I won't go into the chapel. The doorway is shaped like a tombstone, with a red curtain across it. A hand parts the curtain; my little cousin looks out at me. Her fingers are in her mouth. Then she goes away.

My uncle has been to India. He brings us a black bust of Krishna, playing a flute. There's no flute. Krishna is smiling; he has red bracelets up to his elbows.

A Pennsylvania Dutch woman sells us a red and brown rug. I sit in the middle of it. The braids seem to be moving. Each half looks like a house I once lived in. I still see it when my eyes are closed.

I throw some more wood in the stove. (The fire

has gone to ember.) Then I sit back in the rocking chair. For a long time nothing, and then I see the burnt toast. I describe it to Uncle Luis. He walks out of the room. Later he comes back in and sits down. "It's all meat, in God's meat locker," he says.

The toast was gone. There was nothing else to see. My mind itself was silent; there was no wishing there, but a knowledge, right in the center, that I might see it again, know more about it soon, or not soon, and never know it to begin or end. My hands relaxed and I held her lightly; we continued the kiss where we'd left off, and we spent a long time as close as that. She knew I'd seen what I'd seen, but didn't ask. Her neck smelled of cedar-wood fire, balsam, and rosewater. All around there were leaves and moss, inviting, and we would have made love, but when I wanted to, she reminded me of the initiation. (We believed, though it didn't matter much, that it was good to hold on to what's in you, on the eve of important rites.) A little later she forgot that she'd said that, and wanted to make love, and then I had to remind her.

Not much more of the night went by, and no more sounds in it, before the log at the lake was empty of us. Bare feet in moss and eyelids touching, then slowly we separate, mouth from mouth, body from body, hand from hand; she steps to the shore path, as if she'd never stopped her circuit of the water, and I start up the path that climbs out of the vale. There's no sight at all (you have to know the trail), but we both turn once to look at each other. She knows somehow we've been joined. I know I'll see her tomorrow. She goes along with me, up the trail. I stay all night beside her, at Spirit Lake.

Where the trails come together, I gently awakened King Something. He'd let his nose fall down between his knees. We looked down to see that a white mist had covered the lake, and two moons now shone, the one lying low in the sky, and the other, its reflection, on the top of the mist. Then we started home. I told him what had happened; I didn't leave anything out. And I said Spirit Lake was a good place; the feud was meant to end; perhaps someday he'd go down the spur with me. (But he wasn't making any promises.)

Out of the deep woods, back over the Mountain, the only sounds were the horse's hoofs on stones and the song I whistled; it was a toast and a trail song and didn't have words. (You know I'd tell you if it had.) What it did have was notes, and plenty of good empty space between them, filled with images of what I'd seen all night, traces of Lila's smell, and a sensation of almost passive allurement, that seemed compounded of the echo of the notes I whistled, the steps I was stepping, the night passing, and the vision I had seen. And then a fifth thing: the night light on the porch of the farm, at the bottom of the hill, that illumined a small, familiar half circle in the mist, peopled with objects that never changed: the empty cold frame, the shaving barrel, the roses, the four stumps round the campfire stones, the path worn from the farmhouse to the barn.

Come halfway down the hill, below the orchard, King Something paused and beckoned to the right.

He wanted to go to the marijuana garden. So I went along with him; he liked to go there to graze, a few moments at a time, on the leaves and stems passed over in the harvest. I lay down near him as he chewed; the tune I'd stopped whistling stayed on in my mind. The touch of something silk on my hand: I found my fingers lay on a handkerchief covered in dew. It was light-colored, with a picture of the Golden Gate Bridge. I guessed that someone had left it there, on the day the Marijuana Honey-Bee Traveling Air Show came to town.

The
Marijuana
Honey-Bee
Traveling
Air Show

For as long as anyone there could remember, every year on the first of September the Marijuana Honey-Bee Traveling Air Show had come to our farm to perform. It was the happiest day of the summer. The bees themselves decided to do the show for us especially, because the farm was friendly, and because the hill below the peach orchard was big enough for every family in the county to picnic there, and because (the story tells) we were the first farm, ever, to put up marijuana honey.

I won't write very much about it now: it's a day you can probably picture, if you know how a hillside looks under the sun, when it's covered with wildflowers in bloom, and people decked out in their brightest clothes, and children rolling from top to bottom in two's and three's, and old dogs meeting this year's new ones, and, in the middle of all, the great marijuana garden. (You've probably heard songs about it, if you've never been there yourself.) All over the hill, swaying on every flower and alighting to sample their

46

favorite foods (banana bread, bergamot water, peach pie, grits and honey, and sweet-and-sour pineapple), are all the local bees, wild and tame, wanderers and hive-dwellers, of every color and stripe, bees of every persuasion: white clover bees, figwort bees, sunflower bees and mustard bees, Spanish-needle bees, goldenrod bees, sumac bees and boneset bees, basswood and spider-flower and teasel bees, fleabane and heartsease and fire-weed bees, the unctuous buckwheat bees, the hard-working turnip bees, and the marijuana honeybees who live in our own bright-colored boxes. They're all of them quiet, strangely attentive, listening for the first buzz from down over the Beaver Pond, the signal that the Air Show is coming up the glen. As the time approaches, the whole afternoon seems to stand still, from the few clouds above the trees to the hens at the foot of the hill; the storytellers close their word-hoards; old men put down their wine and their eyes are glittering, the children cup their hands over one another's mouths: a long, long quiet and then the first faint buzz from the stand of birch round the pond (fed by the stream, that goes down to the river): at the signal Kamoo the Holy Man himself stands up and hollers, he throws his cap (an old taxi-driver's cap with a plastic visor, and a yellow photograph of him pinned on the peak) up in the air and shouts, the ritual words:

"Here they come, citizens! Like every first of September since the time when the Two were One, coming from Nobody Knows, going to Who Knows Where, jubilizing the brotherhood of man and bee, the fertility of cannabis, and the sweetness of nectar, the Marijuana Honey-Bee Traveling Air Show! I rest my case."

And then sits down again. And the bees in a neat swarm come over the meadow, buzz once around the farmhouse roof, then start up the hill in formation. We have names for all their stunts: Loop the Loop, the Canadian Goose, the Stack, Threading the Needle, Rolling the Barrel, Circle 'Round the Sun, the Wheel of Law, Peeling Off, the Teeter-Totter, the Unfolding Lotus, Engines Off, Pillar to Heaven, and the two sacred dances: the Death of the King, and the Pollination of the Marijuana. For a moment at the end they hover in salute; the local bees rise from their flowers and food; the roar in the air shakes the earth itself, as if a god has awakened from a year-long sleep, and the sky seems to darken. Then just as quickly they're gone, a hum above the horse pasture, the Sugarbush, a whisper over the cemetery. Who knows where? The rest of the day, and most of the night, we eat and we dance. It's September; the golden honey's in jars in the cellar, and the harvest of the plants is soon to come.

I left the scarf on the hill, so it could tell its story to someone else. King Something gladly came along down, to fresh water and hay and his bed in the dark bottom of the barn, and now I'm standing, as on so many nights before, in the small half circle of light before the porch. The light is a lantern, and it flickers in the window like a votive candle set before the Travelers' Saint. We burn it whenever somebody's away. But tonight I feel a vigilance somewhere more than the farmhouse itself possesses, and I crouch and listen a moment on the old stone saddle bench and hum; I do the quick hum called "The Rabbit Erect" to open my ears; slowly there comes the sound of chewing from the West. That's where I look: the moon is a low red circle there, and silhouetted against it I see my father's head; I know his big ears and the baseball cap, the curve of his shoulders and the sound of the chew. He's waiting for me to come home.

Round the shed and into the garden; I pull a carrot from the carrot rows and go to hunker in front of my father; he's got goatskin chaps on his legs and our big American flag wrapped around him (whatever he could find, in the dark, by the door), and his red Philadelphia Phillies cap with a bent-down brim, a couple of golden trout hooks dangling from it, and a button that says "Life is a Dream." (My father was born on April Fools' Day.) I have so many things to say to him that I can't think of one special thing. I smile, and hug him, and think, and he just keeps on chewing. Then I speak:

"That looks like a good radish."

He didn't answer for a long time. First he swallowed what he'd chewed. Then he said:

"They go right through me."

We both added the radish to our thoughts, and didn't speak again till the moon was nearly gone. I could tell our minds were both full, like two buckets of well water you can't pour into each other. I touched his knee but I didn't hurry to speak: I was afraid to. I was afraid, if I spoke, that another illusion would go over the hill with the moon, and not return this time: the illusion that we could kneel there in the radish rows any time, with no need at once to be emptied of all that was in us, just speaking words that came, and letting the rest remain for a while. The picture of us kneeling there under the vanishing moon, subject to no change more rapid than the greening and drying of the weeds, than the slow whitening of hair, than the planting and picking of the radishes, than the soaring and resting of our minds, than the waxing and waning of the moon—that was all an apparition that would go the way of vapor if we spoke the truth both of us seemed to know. That's what it was, and where it went, that night, and soon many words I never said went with it: I never saw my father in moonlight again.

There are two kinds of memories you could have of this scene; one of them is worth forgetting soon, because I don't mean to make you unhappy: if I did, I wouldn't be telling this story. We all still see the moon, and I can still see my father, and want you to see him too, in your own way. We just can't see this moon we see, light up the outline he once had, and throw his shadow on the field. But that's okay. It has to be.

My father looked down to the ground. Pipi was fast asleep, her nose on his foot. I ate half my carrot. I heard him take a chestful of air.

Whenever he took a deep breath, you never knew what to expect. He might say something, or whistle, or just hold the breath and pretend he hadn't breathed it, if anyone was watching. (That was when his heart hurt.) He could whistle like a pine tree. When he was smiling, it didn't take long for the word to travel down the Old County Road on the wind, and whole families would hike up from the Hollow to spend a few minutes with him. He never told anybody what his animal was, but I think it was a trout or a giraffe, because they don't have a song, and nobody anywhere ever heard my father sing, except for one time, and I was there. The sun had gone down on my sister's wedding day; someone lighted the torches and someone else broached the second barrel of applejack, and the first of mead. We all crowded again into the arbor, around the ceremonial bowl I'd carved for the special day. (It was apple wood, full of waves and knuckles; I'd put a ram and a virgin on it, a seaturtle rising from a lotus, a juggling bear, some seashells, a saint whose dress was made of corn, and Buddha as a fishing-boat captain, his face a smile in the rain, his right palm raised, and his left on the tiller, the Wheel of Law.) We brimmed, and toasted, and drained that cup many times, and the faces glowed back at the torches. Someone set the punch afire. Suddenly I grew aware that an unknown voice behind me had started the singing of "Come All Ye Fair and Tender Ladies." It was a voice so honest and delicate that for a moment I was sure it must come from one of the dead ancestors we'd invited (with our opening chant) to the jubilee. I was afraid to turn around; I didn't want him to disappear. Soon everybody knew, and strained to listen:

> *Come all ye fair and tender ladies*
> *Take warnin' how you court your men,*
> *They're like a star, on a summer's mornin'*
> *They'll first appear, and then they're gone.*

A hand found my shoulder; I could feel, from the trembling, that it was the singer's, and I looked down and knew the hand, and then the voice: my father's.

We all joined in on the refrain, and when the last word was sung I turned around to find him gone. He kept to the shadows but I knew where I'd find him, so I didn't follow straight away; I stayed to drink and dance a little more. Later when I went to the Green Room he was still there, right next to the stove, rocking quietly in the dark. He didn't come out all night. I took him some peach pie and later some tea, and saw to it that the stove didn't burn too low. He never sang after that, but he could whistle like a kettle on the fire.

There in the radishes, my father took a breath, and he asked me, "What do you want to be?" (He'd been thinking about that all night.) I hadn't expected him to ask me that, but I thought I knew the answer.

"Everything I am already," I said, "and a Poet, too." (I wanted to grow food and gather food, as we did, and grow poetic images, too, so I could spend my life working close to the unknowable source of both these things—as each image came up, from its sleep in the language, I'd stand aside in wonder, as I do when the shoots of corn break through: "It's corn again!" I holler. "Not the same corn, but it's corn again!")

He thought about that a while. You could tell he was proud. Then he asked me a question: "A poet, hmm?"

"Yes," I said.

"Do you have any words?" he asked. "Gonna need a heck of a lot of words."

I shook my head No. I hadn't thought about that.

"Hmm," he went on (he was concerned), "you can't write poems if you don't have any words. You might as well try to wake up Adam." (That was an expression we had, for something that couldn't be done.)

I wasn't disappointed. I knew that something would come up. I didn't know what I could tell him.

He looked up at the sky, and wrapped the flag a little tighter round his neck. "Winter's coming on," he said.

I nodded my head, and rubbed my chin. There was no denying that. The leaves barely stuck to the trees.

"You never know where we'll be in the spring," he said. Again I had to agree. We had always been right there, but I couldn't think of a reason why we might not be someplace else, come spring. My father was thinking of himself, though; there was a sound on the wind that only he could hear.

"I went down to the Auto-Body Shop today," he said. "Kamoo was working on a blue car."

That really shook me. (He knew it would.) My toes curled deeper into the dirt; I rocked forward on my fists and farted some carrot. News like that always upset me. Once, after I'd eaten a good deal of the mushroom, I was sitting alone on the couch in the Big Room, in the calm not long before dawn. There wasn't a sound for miles. Everyone else was asleep. Suddenly a blue car shrieked to a halt outside the house, the sound of running, and then a man with a big yellow bell burst through the door. He didn't even knock. "There's nobody up but you," he said, "would you ring the bell?" I told him to get the fuck out of here. But that time of night was never quite the same for me; I was always afraid he'd come back.

"We had a talk," my father said. "Kamoo read your chart. He said tomorrow's a good day for your initiation. (I mean today.) There won't be another one till spring, and I could be spirit by then. You never know. You could start on your quest before the next sundown, if you want. That way, if anything happens to me, at least you'll be on your way. The musicians are coming tomorrow, too. And I've got plenty of film in the camera. It'll be a nice day."

It was easy to see he wanted me to go. And I didn't have any reason to stay. He'd never gone on a quest himself ("The father doesn't; the son does"); he'd always been content to sit on the front step and let the people who passed by tell him about theirs. He liked stories, and his smile made the people feel good. The one thing he waited for was the day I would set off on mine, and another thing was the day, if he lived to see it, when I'd at last come home.

I said nothing at all. He knew I had already decided, to pass through initiation that very day. All of the puzzling and preliminary years, since I had come to be known as Silent, had come down to this night that was just about gone.

"Do you have a vision?" he asked. It helped to have one.

I said I did. I told him about the burnt toast. (As much as I knew of it.)

We both sat and thought about the toast. I could almost see it again, over near the tomatoes. Then he spoke up:

"I had a vision too, when I was about as old as you. But I never got the power of it, and I don't have it any more. If you'd like to hear it, I'll tell you. We've got time."

Of course I did. He didn't even have to ask; I'd often wondered if he had one. I crouched even closer to him, and listened as hard as I could. He told me his vision. He didn't leave anything out.

I've had to meditate a long while just now, on whether I can tell you his vision. When I thought I had made up my mind, I went to tell Lila about it.

"Don't be silly," she said. "Of course you can."

This is the story of my father's vision: he was in the West, with my mother; they hadn't known each other long. He'd left his job at the shipyard, and they'd come to visit friends in the Redwoods. Afternoons he'd dive off the coast for abalone, eels, and the big crabs; sunsets he would walk and thumb home to the cabin in the frog meadow, and he'd always meet plenty of deer on the road and beside it. Hilda and Gilda would be sitting on the porch, and Sam (Sam's father) too. American Dave would bicycle home from work at the Clearwater Ranch, and Flew and Richie and Sandy would come up wet from Indian Creek with something good in a bag: thimbleberries or grape leaves, or spearmint or sage.

One evening after supper it was Sam's turn to tell a story. (My father and mother had told all there was to tell about our farm in the Hardwood. Most of what they said would be familiar to you.) Sam talked for a long while. He never told fictions. I know that he seldom spoke, and when he did, it was usually to make forecasts, based on the Book of Changes, which he would open to a certain page, depending upon the ecological data he had received as he'd walked in the forest that day, and along the river, and as he'd breathed and crouched in a special way beneath the plum tree in the back yard. Sam was a plum-blossom numerologist. He was so good at his predicting that he couldn't have cared less if the blossoms were falling or not. It wouldn't even have mattered if the nearest plum tree were on the far side of the coastal range. He'd just look around, and breathe, and then balance both sides of what he'd learned, and then throw out the entire negative half; he'd scatter every pessimistic or hopeless term on the other side of the road; he wouldn't even put them on the compost heap. What was left would be his forecast, and they always came true. (Now that I think of it, I guess it was he who predicted the first destruction of our chimney, and if he'd come round again, he might have predicted the second.)

That night was a specially fine one. Sam was talking about a land where every man knew that he was born to be happy. There was no tension, because there was no contraction within borders; there were no borders, only one fabric, and everything in the fabric was there because it was liked, and lithe men and graceful women were joined in a holy marriage of heat and light, every night, and borne on flowered rattan rafts, by laughing trout, on the six cosmic rivers of Northern California. They'd float downstream, out of the mountains, past happy fishermen who loved to fish, and fish that just loved to be caught, and farms where the two-leggeds played in perfect harmony with the four-leggeds and with the vegetables that stand and think in one place, and wide meadows where teams of friends met to play baseball and capture-the-flag, and between these places, great trees and gullies full of newts, blackberry thickets and the well-worn trails of animals that come from the woods to water. All this was bound to happen, but Sam didn't say just when.

When he sat down, and silence came into the room again, my father leaned back a little, and noticed the slightest of sounds behind him. My mother was leaning over the stove; tears were slowly rolling from her eyes and dropping on to the hot cast iron, where they beaded and hissed and steamed back up to her face. My father worried, and went to her side. He wondered why she was crying.

"It's the moon," she said. "Tonight the moon loses her virtue."

My father stood on the porch and listened to the frogs. He had tried not to think about it; all day as he'd floated on the floor of the sea, waving among the purple fans and the quiet shellfish, he'd tried not to think about it, but still the silver men rode in orbit of the moon, and tomorrow they would land there. My father wondered if he ought to cry. He couldn't tell what the new structure would look like, all he could tell was that the virgin queen, the moon, the huntress chaste and fair, was dressed in a marriage veil of fog. So he stepped from the porch to the yellow weeds, climbed over the wooden fence, passed by the fig trees and the vines of peas, and went for a walk in the red-woods.

He hadn't been walking long when he noticed a strange blue light that seemed to be powder, falling through the tops of the trees, as far around as he could see. It wasn't a light he knew. He heard a sound up ahead, and crept to where he could conceal himself and peer around a great trunk to the source of the sound. What he saw was this: all of the local deer had gathered there, in a clearing—fine bucks and does and fawns that tried to stay in the middle; none of them were very big; they all were covered in the blue-white dust that seemed to glow but not to glitter; they were all looking up to the sky and they were all crying.

My father didn't have to ask them why. He seemed to know, also, that all through the forests of the world, the same rhythmic mourning was going on, as the animals that wander without fear of man, at night, looked up to see their pure friend penetrated. The dark's natural light now fell to the hands of the most predatory creature, he who had once been so afraid of the dark (around him and inside him) that he'd invented fire. At night, at least, he'd gathered in circles round the flames, and the animals learned to live by night, by moonlight. Now, when they looked to the moon, they cried. And the noiseless silver dust fell all around them.

My father ran back to the cabin, stopping for a moment at the sight of the warm light falling from the windows. A man lay in the hammock strung from the house to the plum tree; he was playing a song on a concertina:

> *I'm happy in the summertime*
> *beneath the bright blue sky*
> *No thinkin' in the mornin' where*
> *at night I'll hae to lie*
> *In barn or byre or anywhere*
> *dozin' oot among the hay*
> *and if the weather please me fair*
> *I'm happy every day.*

My father smelled a good smell. "Pancakes," the man said.

"Pancakes?"

"With blackberries in them."

Inside, he joined in the eating. He told what he'd seen. Richie didn't think deer knew how to cry, but everyone else believed. Sam didn't make much of the difference; "That's okay," he said, and then applied his famous Pool-Table Analogy, by which it is shown that in every intentional meeting of people, one person is the foot on the table, and one other is the foot on the floor. He advised my father to throw a change.

The story of the weeping deer ends in a peaceful place: my father kneels with coins on the porch; before each throw he waits a long time, until he feels that the moon and her bursting maidenhead are resting in his hands. My mother sits on the sofa behind him, springs and stuffing coming loose; she's holding a candle. Sam, at the edge of the porch, dangles his feet in the dew on the weeds. A small wind comes and blows plum blossoms on them. They throw the fortieth hexagram, Hsieh, "Deliverance." "The obstacle has been removed. In terms of the Image, thunder—electricity—has penetrated the rain clouds. There is release from tension. The thunderstorm breaks, and the whole of nature breathes freely again." Then there was a change, to the hexagram Tui, "The Joyous, Lake." "When one has penetrated something, one rejoices."

Nobody says a word. The blue snow seems to bring silence with it, mute, and the mutation of forms, in such a way that outlines fall away, or all share the same luminescence: the three are granted a vision beyond the small shape of the moon and the humans hovering there; they see, instead, that the planet's stock of life is free of the planet, the whole breathing freely again. Not soon, but sometime, on some other world far away, some child of a deer or a redwood tree will alight to engender a race that will bloom there in peace and sharing, and stay, or spread, in time that moves fast or slow, long after the last man is gone.

They didn't stay long in the West after that. They came home to the farm in the Hardwood; "returning to the regular order of life after deliverance brings good fortune." My father didn't travel much again; whatever else happened to him after that summer happened mostly right on the farm. He was known to smile most of the time, especially when they caught sight of the Hollow again, after the long trip East, and when they turned uphill at the apple tree and saw, as they started up the Old County Road, that the Squire's long-haired cows still stood chewing in the pasture, as if they hadn't moved, all the months my father had been gone.

After I was born, he sometimes took me fishing, to the lakes not far to the North, full of pickerel and the small-mouth bass, and once skin-diving in the Southern islands; I just found a photograph stuck in a book, I'm holding a great king conch I brought up from a shallow reef, my hair gone blond in front, and my father's standing behind me in a T-shirt, showing off a black-fin tuna. Years ago that was: much later, a short while before this story begins, my father went away for the last time. Not really away; he didn't go but over the first mountain, by himself, to spend a few days with Bob and Sheila, the lightning-bolt makers. Their place was a lot like ours. He stayed longer than he'd planned; he liked it there, and they taught him the trade. He'd just sit with them, all day long, on the front porch making lightning bolts, while the babies played with the ducks in the wallow. Sometimes Sheila would go in the screen door and come out with lemonade and macaroons, and sometimes a man or two would walk by and ask if they could buy a lightning bolt, and Bob would shake his head. If it felt right, he'd give one away, but if not, it couldn't be helped. They were hanging all over the place, from the branches and eaves and the spouts and the flashing. My father brought one home with him, one he'd made himself, and hung it from the maple tree next to the barn. He didn't even mention it. "There are some things you can't talk about," he said. It was a really nice one, but when I tried to compliment him on it, he dropped his shoulders and smiled at his feet. "I'm not very good at it," he said.

My father touched my chest. "So," he said. He pulled up another radish, cleaned it up a bit and took a bite. I rubbed my eyes; the moon had gone down. I had been thinking of the lightning bolt in the tree, but now I thought about Lila, and wondered about her. She would be there tomorrow, my father told me; "They may have gone to get her already."

I wished I could have gone to help carry her off, but that's not the way it was done. ("A woman is brought to the ceremony.") I'd been on several of those parties myself, and it was always a lot of fun. Lila has told me how it was for her:

She tiptoed up to the porch. It was no use; her father was sitting on the swing, pushing lazily back and forth, feet on the railing, chewing and letting fly, cradling a cane in his lap as if it were a shotgun; the two hounds, Angelfoot and Wolfpeach, glared at her from under his seat. The lantern flickered.

"Where you been?" he asked her.

"I've been walking in the Hardwood," she said. She stopped and faced him.

"You smell like a sachet in a drawer full of underwear," he said. She didn't answer. It was a good smell.

"You missed the storytellin' tonight, too. We started *Mount Analogue.*"

"I know," she told him. "I took a walk up the look-out. And then I lay down in the mowing. I came back in time to dance."

Her father had a hunch that some of the Mountain folk were coming for her. He sighted down the end of his cane. "They'll never outshoot me," he said, "they might as well try to stick a hot pat o' butter up a bobcat's ass with a sewing needle." (He must have learned that one at the sawmill. One of the guys at the mill had a wife who worked at the Book Press.)

Lila didn't play with him. "There hasn't been a gun up on the Mountain since the time when the Two were One," she said.

"Everything changes," he said. "Lot of peddlers coming through this time of year." He sighted all along the ridge, East to West, West to East; he didn't miss a thing. (There wasn't much to see: it was perfectly dark; the only light anywhere was the lantern two feet from his head.)

"I'm going to sleep," Lila said. She kissed him in the ear, then went into the house, into her room. The squeak of springs. The picture on the wall. She let herself doze; in an hour or two she'd be up to meet my friends on the ridge.

Her father went to bed. His spit dried on the stone.

"So," my father said again, swallowing, "that was my vision."

I nodded my head. It was a good one. Now I knew why I was born a deer.

He tried to explain why he hadn't gone on a quest after that, but I stopped him with my hand; it's understood that all visions lead you home; only some of them carry you away at first, lead you to turns and chances and lost ways, too many to name, before they bring you home. He didn't have to explain.

He looked up where I'd just looked. "Moon set," he said.

"Yes." My hand on my chin. My eyelids rest.

"You should go to bed," he said; there wasn't much night left. He was going to stay out a few minutes longer.

We both stood up. My knees complained a little less than his. He put his arm around my shoulder. (He was taller by an inch.) We didn't really look at each other then; both of us looked instead, together, at the house across the field, warm and vigilant, the Hardwood all around it. The porch lantern glowed and now the light in the kitchen had gone on, as if, in a way forever out of time, we were sitting there too, at the table by the stove, drinking camomile tea in silence, while this evening's shadow version of ourselves played in the radish rows. And now in the field

the moon had set, and we were about to go join those waiting in the kitchen. I hugged my father (never pass up a chance to hug somebody), our eyes met, and then I set off toward the house. When I had just reached the end of the cucumbers, he called out to me, one last word:

"Hey!" he called; I stopped and turned around. Even though there was no light but that from the porch and the kitchen, I seemed to see him perfectly; he'd moved a few steps to his right, into the weeds; he'd dropped the sheepskin and the flag, and stood now clad in nothing but the bright red baseball cap, and a giant burdock leaf he was holding against him, that covered him from his thighs to the top of his belly, which was just beginning to go a little soft. And his face was one great smile, that lifted his cheeks out to his ears, and closed in on his glowing eyes.

I floated over the last cucumbers; I knew what he was saying to me, and I felt as happy as I can ever be.

"That's okay, that's good!" I called, and then I couldn't see him any more. The light in the kitchen had gone out.

Kathy was in the kitchen. She had turned the light on, and then she'd turned it off. She was undressed, facing away from me, on her knees before the stove; the back and the top of her beautiful thighs were what I saw first, coming into the kitchen, and now that I was close to her I watched her breasts swing in the orange light of the fire (and the fire-shadow of her breasts on her thighs), her glistening lips, her white hands on the iron poker. She looked up at me, eyes wide; she wasn't surprised.

"Noodle woke me up," she explained, "so I'm baking a raisin pie."

I got down on my knees beside her. Our sides touched and we put our arms (my left and her right) on each other's back; we opened the oven and looked at the pie. It was just growing big in the middle, and golden where the crust hung over the pan. She didn't have to tell me what was in it; I could smell every thing, each time I breathed: raisins, slices of ginger root, nutmeg and clove, sunflower seeds, orange peel, sesame, cinnamon; one of Kathy's pies.

"It's almost done," she said. "I carved your name on the crust."

It was true. She really had. And someone had

washed my overalls; they hung from the damper on the stovepipe, steaming. We looked at each other for a long, long time. Tomorrow I was going away.

After a while she spoke again:

"The stove's pretty hot, if you want to have a bath."

So I went to the barn and brought back eight sugaring pails, filled them from the tap in the kitchen, set them on the stove to cook. It was a good idea.

Kathy took out the pie. She laid it on the floor between us. "It should cool a little bit," she said. I put some wood on the fire, and then we faced each other, the pie between four knees; threads of steam and sometimes sweet bubbles rose from the SILENT she'd etched on the top; the steam disappeared when it reached our chins. I forgot where I was for a moment (I do that a lot), and thought I'd been born inside the pie, letting bursts of melted spices out through my name. One could do worse.

"Would you like to cut the pie?" she asked me.

I shook my head. I'd get the milk. I'd get the cream, too. Cups. And dishes.

What we didn't eat (and we ate a lot, very slowly) we put up in the warming oven, wrapped in a dish towel. I went to pour the bath. Floated in the tub, only my eyes and nose above the water. Kathy brought a lantern in, and she sat beside the tub. She sat (carefully: splinters) on an old wooden crate with a nice picture on it. It was a picture of an artichoke with a big grin, wearing three-fingered white gloves, tipping his straw hat, one of his patent-leather shoes on the solid ground, and the other high in the air, near his other hand, which was waving. There were hundreds of similar artichokes in the field behind him, and a blue sky above, filled with musical notes. Underneath him was a caption: "Artichoke Capital of the World." There was nothing in the crate. It was for sitting on, and that's what Kathy was doing.

"Can I get in with you?" she asked me. I put my hand up to her. I had been hoping she would. She gave me a long massage, and then I gave her one. We used oil of wintergreen this time, and all our strokes (even on the soles of our feet) moved toward the heart. There's a special way to do it; you should learn it from someone who knows. When we had finished and all our muscles were quiet, we kissed, a long taste of her mouth and raisin pie, inside silky and wet as the outside. She came around behind me, under my back she lay and put her arms around my chest, so that we both faced the ceiling, and the back of my head floated on her breasts, that rose and fell like the ocean. Her voice a whisper behind me:

"Silent," she said, "aren't you ever going to speak to me?"

I felt bad about that. I hadn't meant not to speak to her, just nothing had come up. So I started to think of something good to say, for her only, but before I had a chance to, the touch of her breathing breasts on my head lifted me one last time, half out of the water, and slowly dropped me down to sleep.

I don't remember getting out of the bath, and going to bed, but a few images came to my mind when I tried to remember, and they're probably true (it doesn't matter: anything that happens at that hour of night is a dream): I rise from the tub and go to my room; I don't dry. I leave a still trail of steam where I pass through: the Ivy Room, the kitchen, the pantry, the Big Room, the stage, the stairs, the loft. The steam is slow to dissipate; it's still there when Kathy follows through, carrying the lantern, crosses to her bed off the greenhouse (she loves plants), and falls asleep. Just once on the way, when her trail turns from mine, she pauses to look up, and that's when I look down; she lifts the lantern near her face, with care she blows the steam (four-colored smoke of the sacred red willow bark) in the four cardinal directions: East, where morning's soon to be; South, over the mountain, from where I've just come home; West, to the land of the dead, where I must go (if I want); and North, to Adam's Ear, from where I'll return. She disappears from where they meet, and I know two things, lying down: all of my body breathes, slowly and deeply, the sun in my arms, while the small center in me, still awake, wills to dream the dream that sounds my departure.

The
Cucumber
Theory
of the
Universe

My father shows me the house where he was born. It's not in the Hardwood; it's in the town, facing the market square. We come down the sidewalk close to the wall, trying to keep out of the rain. The torn posters on the wall: concerts by young conductors, the carnival across the river, recycle used paper, a meeting of citizens concerned—we stop before his house. They have made it into a brothel. We peer through the window (the Italian wrought-iron screen, the gauze curtain): a woman lies in a bed of ostrich feathers. I'm bending over her; my lips hide her nipple from view. We strain to see. We stand in the room.

My father tells me how soon he means to die.

"Go mix with the crowd," he says. I sing him a song. It goes like this:

> *I'll be your ghost,*
> *we'll call on girls, they'll know*
> *to open knees a little wider*
> *because I'm coming*
> *with my father.*

We look out the window. A junkman has taken shelter under the awning. He has an antique valve trombone on his cart, with a bullet hole in one bend. Some of the ladies go outside to buy jewelry from him. They make him gay with their attention. He likes to be a junkman. We can hear them laughing. My father is not sure we're in the right house. He thinks he knows the fountain, the flowers round it, the kiosk, the statue of the Indian on a horse, holding his arms out sadly, the steps on which the two old people stop to speak under an umbrella.

Somewhere else perhaps; he's sure he can find it. The entrance to a large estate. The rain's much harder, and we stand under an oak tree. It's dark. We're near the small bright window of the thick-walled gatehouse, where the keeper and all his family sit around the fire. It reminds us of home. The rain will be bad for the harvest, if it keeps up. Sacks full of them, come up yellow and soft. A bad day, a bad year, for cucumbers.

"**T**here's pink grapefruit," my father said, shaking my foot. It wasn't raining at all; the sun filled the room. It had just come up. My father was sitting on the end of the bed, in his red and black lumberjack shirt that he knew I liked to see him in; in his lap lay Thorn, our ceremonial ax. He'd opened the window wider; the cool October air came in. I awoke a little:

"Pink grapefruit," I said.

"Hash browns and fried eggs, too. And barley bread. I just had some." It was true. I could smell them.

I lay still for a while. He played with my knee. I could tell that he hadn't slept since I'd left him in the garden; I could always tell that: he'd look me in the face and whistle like a truant; it wasn't a thing he talked about. We listened to the sounds outside: some calling birds, the water, maple leaves falling, the roar from the bottom-land.

I worried about the roar.

My mother leaned into the room, in her green velour robe. "It's the train," she said, "they're warming it up," and went to cook an egg.

My father was happy. He held up the ax, a double blade on a long ash handle, cut from a lower branch of the Great Ash itself, in a far-off part of the Hardwood. "First we'll cut the tent pole," he said. "What kind of tree will it be?"

I answered right away. A birch tree. I'd always wanted it to be a birch tree.

"I'll be downstairs," he said, and went out of the room. Then he came back for a moment, I thought he had something else to say, but I guess he didn't. He just looked once round the room, the window, the several books, the painting, me in the bed. He went downstairs.

Then I did something I sometimes do. It's a trick I

learned from Rita the Hypnotist, who sometimes appeared down at the Hollow. Word would come up the Old County Road, and I'd run down to fetch her (all the dogs would run there with me), because she walked with a little limp and liked to have me hold her arm on the way uphill. One of her daughters would have fixed her golden hair in a special way, and round her neck she wore chains of cameos and sea stones, polished crystals and petrified redwood. She carried a string bag from her shoulder; inside it was a talking metal parrot that didn't work (no batteries); it was perched on a pink cypress knee that said, in gold glitter, "In the Beginning Was the Word." Everyone on the farm loved Rita; we'd all lie down in the meadow when she came, and we'd concentrate on her words and one of her stones. She'd talk for a long while, with many silences, and then she'd lie down too. Some of those times I'd smile so hard my face would hurt. She'd always give the same two suggestions: You are what you want to be, and, All evils of life vanish for him who keeps the sun in his heart.

One day in the peach orchard she taught me a trick. We were talking about praiseworthy spaces, the spaces that poems tell about. "The most praiseworthy one of all is your body, Silent, did you know?" she asked me, and I said, I'd always thought so. I put my thumb on my lower lip. "Would you like to meet the inside of you?" she said. I'd be delighted.

"You can do this yourself anytime," Rita told me, and she introduced me to my toes. And then my feet, my ankle bones and calves, all the way up to my head. I don't know how to tell you how it felt. She smiled down at me, and I up at her. "You're everywhere," she said. (In Rita, in the peaches.) I looked around. It was true. "And some of you's inside here" (tapping my chest); "when you die it'll be like having your fingernails cut. It won't be anything more."

That's what I sometimes do in the morning, especially if I have special things to say. So for a few minutes I stayed in my bed and said hello to all the parts of me (I'll just name a few): my toes, that had sunk in the warm moss by Spirit Lake; my legs, that still felt the touch of Lila's thighs across them; my cock, that lay loose and contented all the while Kathy rubbed me and then when I rubbed her (for such repose, many Hindoo ascetics have pored through Patanjali's sutras, till their flesh tails the ravens downwind); (thinking about it now, the muscle starts to stir—you never can tell when it will); my chest, that breathed with delight and let forth words; my nose (I never forget my nose); my mouth; my mind, that watched and set all these things down to tell, including this very sentence.

I oiled my mountain boots, and put them on, and then my overalls and a red bandana round my neck. I started down to the kitchen. My sister was coming down too. (She's a little older.) She kissed me good morning, and as she did, she pressed something into my hand.

"For later," she said. "Don't look at it now," and I put it in my pocket.

My father put his hand on my shoulder. I was sitting down. He asked me a question:

"Do you think you should eat before your initiation? Think about it a while. It's up to you."

I didn't have to think very long. I was hungry.

He stood there while I ate. I guessed his other hand was in his pocket, playing with his little black-and-white chapstick. I'm a slow eater. I had a second cup of tea.

That's when we opened the farmhouse door, and went outside. A great snowy owl took off from the nearest tree, and disappeared over the barn. He didn't say anything. That's when we walked toward the out-house, and the two dogs and Rosemary, the goat, started up the long hill, and we saw the few peaches left in the orchard, and I woke up the animals. We sat a few minutes in the outhouse.

I rocked my chin up and down.

"Last night was a good one," I answered.

I was finished. I fastened my overalls. He was finished, too. He pulled up his pants. Just before he did, and we went out to cut the birch tree down, I glanced at his cock. It was a pretty big one.

"You should widen that second hole before you go," my father said.

It's no use trying to tell you all that happened that morning, in any order; though it was a long morning, and people had things to do, it seems like a moment to me, something I saw as I sat up in the peach or-chard, opened my eyes and looked around, and closed them again very soon. In fact, if you want to think of me as sitting there in the orchard, not going anywhere really (just watching, like you) from the first sign of morning till the last word of this story is told, you can do that; it's up to you. Memories are motionless, anyway. If what I've told you until now has given you the illusion that we've moved in ordered time, and that's how you know me, that's okay, but as for me, I reckon I will be sitting in the peach orchard (every farm has a place like this) high on the hill, and you're beside me (we can learn more that way); we're all as motionless as these words, that do nothing but set in motion the thing between us.

I look down at the places most intimate to me, in the field determined by the bend in the Old County Road, where it disappears by the cemetery, and in the opposite direction, the great apple trees beyond the garden, and the third point: the orchard itself, the start of the path through the Sugarbush, over the Mountain to Spirit Lake. Many memories of the morning are fixed in that space; to see or to picture the pumpkin patch, the shingles stacked by the chicken house, the red door, the place I was born in, between the acres of rye, the tire dangling from the tree, is to see or to picture the people suspended there (sometimes I'm one of the people), doing what they did, without duration. Each time they glance my way, I fix them more securely in their space, rescued from sequence, which melts things away.

We cut a dead silver birch, up by the upper well. We roll it downhill. My father wants to rest halfway down, so we sit by the blueberry island. (Once Raymond almost mowed the berries down; we had a new cutter-bar and he got carried away. Michael came running up the hill, waving his arms. "What's up?" Raymond shouts. He can't hear him 'cause the tractor's going.) We watch the people setting up the tent. Kathy comes out the door and looks around. When

74

she sees us she waves. Then she goes back in the house. My mother makes a bargain with Michael. He brings three more pumpkins from the patch. The four musicians come over the Mountain. Lila pokes her head from an upstairs window; someone pulls her in again. The people stand under the apple tree with baskets and I shake the fruit from the tree. We carry them to the press. I kneel before the spout. The cider bursts against my face. Forty gallons in the barrel. The tent's raised on the tip of the birch tree, and the old men file in. My grandmother hands something through the door, and then my father approaches the tent in his cloak, carrying his camera in a purple string bag. He pitches his spear into the ground and gives the five-note whistle. They let him in. Kamoo the Holy Man comes up the road, his clothes stained from the Auto-Body Shop. When he reaches the crossroad, he sets the falcon free. He hands out magic mushrooms to everybody but me. "Don't get excited," he says. "Drink this," and I do. It tastes like weasel piss. He watches my face change; then I'm above him. He shouts up at me: "You'll feel like nine movie stars! I rest my case." He goes to spend some time with Lila. I lie down. The people surround me. Kamoo sticks his head out the window: "Paint him up good!" he hollers. Kathy begins to undress me. She watches my penis rise toward her. Our smile. Oil of cedar, juniper berries. They make me up to look like the Musketaquid River. The blindfold, and then Kathy's voice in my ear: "You mustn't speak." (As if I would.) They bear me to the tent. Someone says the words. The inspector comes out: "Is this the world traveler?" he asks. I feel myself blush beneath the grease. The examination's over; "Let him through," he says. Shouting and chanting and whistles, and then the music starts, loud to waken the ancestors, to tell them to spread the news in the other world. ("He who can wholly comprehend this sacrifice can rule the world as though it were spinning on his hand.") Waves of drums and laughter; my bones tremble. The tent full of smoke, smell of birch wands steaming. They bind my wrists to the pole. The growing roar.

A hand touches my chest. The noise cut off. Kamoo will speak.

I don't want him to speak just yet; his hand feels good there. So I'll tell you something about him, Kamoo the Holy One, the Black Maharishi, proprietor of the Peerless Five-Walled Auto-Body Shop, magician and dealer. He's not a shaman.

"I'm a sky pilot," he says, "came up the hard way."

He came by his power in a way worth telling. He wanted to cross the wide Missouri. It was March. He fell in with a band of gypsies who were heading West; (gypsies always head West), and they left him off somewhere in the Dakotas, but not before he'd dishonored one of their women. The wagon wasn't going very fast, and while he slept she rolled him over the side, lest he expose her shame round the campfire: words came to him all too quickly. He awoke by the light of the moon, but there was little to see—plains and the far-off buttes, some tumbleweed, a snow fence, the wind rattling a stovepipe down the road. He went to investigate. Perhaps a house.

The whole front wall a billboard: BADLAND BONES. SEE the DINOSAUR EGG. (Closed until spring.) He broke in a window. Nothing to eat, no money in the till, no till, a mattress for sleeping behind the souvenirs. Fossils and bones on the shelves, a mastodon tusk, a big footprint, a diorama of some Indians chasing a beast, the beast caught in tar, spears (cocktail toothpicks) in his side, the sagebrush made of bits of yellow sponge. Kamoo went to sleep.

He was awakened by a curious spectacle. The moon came bright through the windows and the room filled with sound. He peeked over the counter. When he saw what he saw, he wished he were someplace else, huddled outside by the water tank, riding the legs of the gypsy woman, back across the Missouri, getting stoned in the rear of his father's Auto-Body Shop. Anywhere but there, in a shack on the plain, where the March wind made dust of the buffalo bones outside, and inside:

The fossils had joined hands and were trucking on the Southern shelves, and the trilobites and saber teeth were rattling the display case on the west wall, and near the door the big bones were dancing an unnameable dance, all of them shrieking, but not together. Kamoo crouched rooted where he was, his eyes wide, his nose resting on a plaster ashtray in the shape of a big-breasted squaw who took the butts in her lap. There were seven more just like her, all in a row. Suddenly all the noise ceased; the bones stood still: on the pedestal in the middle of the room, the Dinosaur Egg was about to speak. He only speaks once every ten million years, so whenever the Dinosaur Egg opens up his word-hoard, everybody shuts up and listens; it's bound to be something important. Kamoo listened well, and he didn't forget a word (so he says); he wrote it down in the morning, and sang

it all the way home, traveling with a troupe of itiner-
ant preachers. It became the first hymn in his book,
Hymns for Sky Pilots, which sold well in the East, and
brought us down the Old County Road to seek his
services, and whenever we ate a mushroom of his, or
sniffed the dust or swallowed a cup of his potion
("Gypsy Juice," he said) and asked where he got his
power, he'd always answer, "from 'The Ballad of the
Dinosaur Egg.' I rest my case."

The Ballad of the Dinosaur Egg

Gonna plug in my season machine
Make the summer white, make the winter green.
If you sleep all night in the fossil room
You'll hear the Dinosaur Egg sing his song of gloom,
It's a tale of doom:

Never was great, never was green,
Dinosaur birds never pecked me clean
Don't ask me why I'm so forlorn
My folks were extinct before I was born.

> *So don't cast my footprint*
> *Don't set my leg*
> *I'm not a dinosaur*
> *I'm a dinosaur egg.*

When my father knew he was bound to die
I was a tear in his terrible eye
He was afraid his last dinosaur snatch
Would turn into stone, and never hatch.

With her dying moan Ma parted from me
(Some monkeys looked on from the limb of a tree)
Then she died all alone in the cool of the mud
Never a human drew dinosaur blood.

    So don't stone my brow
    Don't stab my leg
    I'm not a dinosaur
    I'm a dinosaur egg.

The darkness came over my father's pea-brain
Like the ice in the air where there once had been rain
He fought with the strength of forty-two men
But the mighty walk once, and never again.

    So take me to the corner
    Leave me there to beg
    I'm not a dinosaur
    I'm a dinosaur egg.

When Death flings his mantle over the skies
You don't need a brain of a wonderful size
To know that all of the works you've begun
Could turn into stone, along with your son.

    So don't point your finger
    Don't slap your leg
    I'm not a dinosaur
    I'm a dinosaur egg.

"Brothers and sisters, look at Silent's eyes." Kamoo took off my blindfold so they could see. As for me, I looked but saw nothing; Kamoo had fed me the creeper to slow me down, and all I could see or hear was a great blur (I was a cactus trying to focus on a hummingbird), except for the drawl of Kamoo, and the swimming move of my father's pale-blue robe, as he glided among the speeding company, taking photographs for the Mountain Book.

"Look into his eyes," he went on. "They glitter like chunks of crystal on the river bed at noon." I looked up at him; he was a little hard to see; sparks seemed to fall lazily from around his head. I decided that most of these things were secrets, and I would pass over them, if ever I told this story.

"I've known this young man since the day he was born. The story of that day's well-known: the horned owl flew over the acres of rye and dropped a deer's hindquarters right in the boiling water, just spittin' distance from where his father and I were sitting, holding his mother's hands, ain't that right?"

My father said yes. It happened that way.

"We'd been dancing and smoking all night in the fields. The first thing he saw was the sunrise, and the moon going down. The sun in Leo, the moon in Aquarius, Cancer rising. We waved him above the rye, that was green and just about as big as he was. He's what they call a cottontail deer."

Kamoo said a lot more things. He told the ritual tale of how life had been before the feud, when the two farms were one, and the great front porch where everyone rocked at sunset, the May Days, the music, the trips, the salads, blazing trails in the dense Hard-wood, raising cairns on the Mountain, pulling up stumps in the field. And then the first hesitant arguments about Time: to measure or not, to fill it with a singleness that expands and seeks the simplest shape, or to try to outguess the time to come, to criss-cross it with a structure, beams and joints and timbers in the midst of nothing, and no place to fall. The old man who stood to speak, finally, on the last night. He didn't deny anything. It's true; the heart thinks constantly; this cannot be changed. But the movements of the heart should be restricted to the immediate situation. "All thinking that goes beyond this only makes the heart sore." The sad leave-taking. Half the people move down to the lake. In time the reasons are forgotten, but the two remain two. The dead are buried in each place.

Kamoo led a hymn, the one about the lily pad floating on the water. "Look at this boy," he said, "the one made up like the river. Wherever he goes, he smiles and sings and people automatically make way. If you're patient he'll carve a little canyon right before your eyes. He's hardly touching the ground! Look at the smile on his face: you'd think his big toe had just been pierced by an arrow from the sugar-cane bow, with the bowstring of murmuring bees. He moves with ease in both worlds; ten pairs of tortoises can't stop him; he's what they call a V.D.C., a Very Decent Citizen. Look into his eyes and see the mountain above, the lake below: simplicity outside, power inside. And look all around you; it's the time they call Decrease: the sun's gone South, the temperature's dropping, the sap in the maples won't rise until spring, the snow's going to fall, yet Silent's about to undertake something. He can't wait another day! And he can't fail; he understands the time; all the oracles just have to say so; his luck is assured. So I've heard. Now he's at rest; he's on his back, and he'll stay at rest while he moves; he'll move through the world and not see in it the struggle of individuals, the spruce trees will bend down and brush the flies from his head, and he'll learn the meaning of the mystery of Burnt Toast." (When he said the name, the people all murmured. I heard them do that.)

"But in fact he already knows what the burnt toast is, don't you, Silent?" I nodded my head. I guess I did.

"The quest is just a structure, like anything else." That was true. I was aware of that. People who stayed, and people who went away, found out the same truth, more or less. We even had special names for the two kinds of people, but the names were never used. "It's over before it begins." That was not really true, I thought: I didn't have any words, and I needed to go find some, so I could be a poet.

"Look at his forehead," he finally said, "it's already glowing, as if the dualities are gone, and the Two are One. The middle of his brow is shining, as if the jewel's already there. He leaves the Mountain, but he comes back. I rest my case."

The rest of the initiation I can't tell much about, except for the drumming, and it's hard to write about drumming. They chanted many of my favorite chants. I knew my mother's voice, and Kathy's. Gradually the people began to slow down, and I made out their faces through the steam and smoke, and the paint round their mouth and eyes. I didn't have to be told I was in good company, gathered from the Mountain and from other farms in the county, elders whose eyes didn't waver, young men who'd lain where I lay, not long since; I remembered how many times I'd seen the same group mustered in the great pavilion in the Hollow, or gathered below the peach orchard, on the hill.

The four musicians played the circumcision song. I can't tell you how it's sung, but the words are something like this:

> *Out of the hardwood comes the doe*
> *Kneel down drink at the river*
>
> *Up comes the sun behind her head*
> *Give her all the light it can give her*
>
> *The river runs along her tongue*
> *Sunlight bursts in the water*
>
> *Jump up fish, splash of her hoof*
> *The doe is the uncle's daughter.*

Lila came in the tent then. She was dressed up to look like a cottontail deer, but I recognized her; I knew her smell, the way her thighs moved, her arms not thin, the way the people danced to reflect her when she crossed the threshold; in her right hand she held the small ceremonial knife we use, with the red and blue streamers hung from the hilt. I was excited to see her, you could tell if you looked at me closely, but all in all, I wouldn't want to go through it again; once is plenty; they'd never get me in there a second time. And it's been proved to me many times since, in gentler ways, too many to name, that there are equal lots of pleasure and pain in this world, and the happy man is he who walks among them thinking, "The Self is not affected by this."

The musicians continued the song, without words; the elders hopped up and down, crying the cries of the animals they embodied. (All their animals were extinct; the voices lived on in the elders alone.) The torches were all doused; the room became a great black, smoke-filled space, as if my blindfold now surrounded everything. Kamoo began the circumcision chant. The people picked it up. Lila stood between my legs, bent over me, her left forearm on my chest, her right hand near my thigh, grasping the ceremonial knife. She took my cock between her lips. Her mouth was as soft as a clam. She moved slowly up and down. (She seemed to know how to do it pretty well, but I always try not to ask the wrong question.) My chest moved up and down exactly with her, as if it was really breath we were exchanging, and now words leave me: there's just this picture left, that only she and I (and now you) see, in the black inside the tent: we're together a long time; she hums deep in her throat and my hips rise toward her; my hands grip the powdery birch tree, the rest of me falls loose—as if by instinct I cry out, the sacred four-syllable shout, to let her know it's happening; the musicians hit the loudest chord and the people hold the note of their chant and the long animal wails, and as I burst she brings the knife against me, makes the small incision (not very big at all; it's just a symbol) on the bottom of my cock; some blood falls (pretty much for such a little cut, I think), the ground soaks it up, the initiation's over. There's half an hour of silence, and then we chant. My mother and father and sister come around me.

The great feast, after, in the house: garlic soup, salad, brown rice and vegetables, corn fritters, goat cheese, pumpkin bread, apple cider, mince pie, and tea.

Once during the meal I reach as far as I can to get some wild grape jelly for my bread. I hesitate a few seconds over the jar, and the jelly slowly slides off the fork, back where it came.

Lila leans close to me:

"You had time," she says, "it would have fallen right on to the bread."

I nod my head.

"I know. That's what I should have done."

A little later: Kathy and I outside, walking around the house. Her arm a loop in mine. She puts her tongue in my ear. She'll be here when I come back, she whispers, and I let her know that's good, that's what will bring me home. Very soon, too; "not a long old time." We walk around again. Rosemary the goat's eating the paper sign someone once put up: "All Hail to the One Cosmic Mind." The last word is just disappearing into her mouth. She'll eat anything.

"Will you be back in time for the end of the story?" Kathy asks.

"I hope so," I answer. "Whatever happens."

We jump the mill stream. The mud on the other side. We stand under the Golden Delicious apple tree, a long while listening to the sounds from the house.

We eat some apples off the ground. She holds my hand when she bends down. Some soft ones we throw across the road, into the woods. I throw one of them really far, down the road; it rolls under the wheels of a panel truck just coming over the rise. It's the *Dream-Fluff* Do-Nut truck. The driver turns the engine off, hops out, and takes a piss on the signpost. He's got a nice new hat on.

"That's some hat," I call out, and he comes over.

"It is, isn't it? They're handing them out down at the Good-Will store." It's white, with an emblem on it: a picture of a mug full of root beer, with little drops of condensation coasting down the sides.

"Would you like a doughnut?" he asks us.

I'd like one. "I'll take a Honey-Dipt," I tell him.

Kathy wants one too. "A Balkan Cream-Filled." We walk around to the back of the truck. Inside there's a man asleep on a pile of sacking, wrapped in a yellowed sheet, the oldest man I've ever seen, the hair gone from his head and his long beard in the doughnuts.

"I picked him up down at the Hollow," the driver explains.

I touch his knee to waken him, and lean next to his face, so he can see me. He smells like a goat.

He sits up. He slaps the top of his head, really hard.

"Where are we?" he asks.

"We're here," I tell him. I look to Kathy. She nods her head; it's true.

"His name's Haroon," the driver says, handing us our doughnuts.

"Ah." We take bites.

"Has the storytelling started yet?" the old man asks.

"No it hasn't. You're just in time, in fact."

He was happy to hear that, because he had a story to tell.

"It's a long one," he said, "and I'd like to start today. It's the last one I'll ever tell."

Kathy took his arm and we started back to the house. "We're very anxious to hear it," she said.

I held out my hand to the Do-Nut man. "Why don't you come too," I said.

He put his hand on his cheek. "Don't mind if I do," he replied, and started after us. Then he ran back to the truck, disappeared in the back, and came out with a bulging sack. "Doughnuts," he explained. "I baked them myself, while you were asleep." I looked at Kathy, and she looked at me: we hadn't been asleep then.

We three crossed at the footbridge, but the Do-Nut man decided to leap the stream. He took a running start. One hand holding the sack on his shoulder, the other on top of his hat; his legs open like a scissors above the stream. The light through red and yellow leaves, music from the house. He makes it to the other side. A cloud of powdered sugar settles slowly to the water.

We cleared away the dishes and lifted the old man on to the platform where the Monkey-Ward stove used to be. He balanced himself on his sawed-off thornwood stick, that seemed to be carved, with figures you'd recognize (perhaps with fear) if you got up close. He let the yellowed sheet fall from his shoulders (it fell into pieces when it hit the ground), revealing a body gone blanched and dry, covered only by a stained piece of loincloth that the Rag-Man of the Highway would have walked right by. It seemed to be pinned to the skin of his hips.

I told my grandmother how he'd come.

She parted her shawl a little. "The world has many turns," she said.

We all ate our doughnuts and awaited his first words. It was always a momentous thing, when a man told his last story. It usually meant that he had come to see clearly, just before death, that a dominant theme ran through all of his stories; from the first, that began with riddles the young man didn't understand, to the last, in which he joined, as a single structure, all of the stories he'd ever told. And the composition of the audience was important, representing the teller's potential to live on. So I looked around the room, and felt that powerful sense among the people; we all gathered closer to the platform, like silent, experienced hikers in the woods, who stop and stand around a spring, ringed by stones, where a long underground river bursts through the surface for a moment, then passes on below.

Lila whispered something to me:

"The train won't leave without you?" she said.

"No," I told her, "the conductor's right here." And he was: Uncle John was sitting on the floor, leaning against the woodpile, a great calabash dripping with applejack on his lap, his cap down on his nose, and his left hand round an ankle of Verandah, who was warming her fingers above the stove.

It's often been said (the old man began), and rightly so, that every man builds himself a house inside his mind. He grows intimate with it as he grows, and fills the house with daydreams, dreams, and memories, and when he goes there in reverie or in deepest slumber, he moves among objects, and in spaces, that have come to mean more than their name would imply: the chipped bowl before the window, with one golden hair wound in the bottom, may contain all the memories of a particular winter, or the names of all the animals in the zoo by the lake, and the touch of a hand, or the seven meanings of a famous tale—all the objects in the house, and the house itself, are but places where a catalogue is kept, a memory system to shelter and to integrate a man lost in the cosmos. Sometimes he stands motionless, looking out, the house a refuge in night or winter; sometimes he lights the smoky lantern and goes down in the dark cellar, keep of the memories he was born with, and the first dreams and images of being housed; very little light comes in, perhaps one slanted window plastered with old leaves, a highlight on the wet beneath a pipe. In all the house there's nothing that he wouldn't want to see.

I ask you to look into this jewel; think of what you see there. (The old man held up a jewel, and this is what I saw: red and purple mountains, covered in mist, two people walking in the pouring rain. Their feet catch in the mud of the road. They glance behind. A wind lifts the coat of one. A woman. The rain is just a curtain, behind it a blazing sun; the mountains and the couple disappear. A clay house in a clay-house village, yellowness of noon: a bald old man steps from

his door and dumps a small pot of dirty water; the
ground soaks it right up; a skinny dog races from the
shade across the street and licks the wet place. The
man shades his eyes to look in the shimmering distance. He goes back into the house.)

The old storyteller went on: That man's name is
Haroon the Jar-Man; you may think of him as me. He
was a maker of great clay pots; he gathered and
wedged the clay himself near one of the purest wells
of the oasis, not many steps from his door; moreover,
his fame as a memory-technician had spread far
beyond the four gates of the city, though there's very
little out there. People came to him to buy his pots
(he made very few of them) and for advice on how to
compose the space in their memory ("fixations of happiness," he'd say), so that he lived as well as most did
there.

Time passed. (It does.) He left behind the age
when most men have accumulated about all the
memories they need and, finding the complex burden-
some, begin to shed the ones on the surface, as a
snake sheds his skin when it becomes too tight for
him to move. So his memory house was very simple:
the four walls, bare but for one picture of the name of
God, the window (toast-shaped) that gave on to the
date palm, the counter, the bowl, the ladder to the
roof, his two finest pots on the shelf: one of them
with a figure of a bluebird with a crescent moon for
an eye, and a terrible crack that ran from the lip to the
base; the other a little smaller, with a red and yellow
flower, and two smooth handles on the hips; and, last,
a cast-iron hook near the door, where Haroon knew
he'd hang the walking stick, when it finally came to
his hands. He'd learned that in a dream.

What visions these objects contained, I need not tell you, but for the two clay pots on the wall. The first, the larger one, was his wife. (He'd met her when he was already old.) He had refined his memory of her to one image, which he kept in the jar: the image of a well (the Well of the Wild Asparagus) in moonlight, and himself asleep beside it, dressed in black, his hands cupped on the clay with which he would make this very jar. (Though years have gone by, whenever he sleeps, he sleeps in this position.) It was at that clay-pit, by that well, that he met his wife, and it was there as well that he went to sleep on the night she died; she broke bearing his daughter.

His daughter was the second jar ("my finest vessel," he said). Anyone who looked there, and heard him speak those words, would certainly have told him that there was no vessel there, because that was the truth; the jar was gone. One day he'd awakened and found just a piece of it on the floor. His daughter was nowhere to be seen. He put the piece back on the shelf. Two dreams which he'd recently had (he thought) he put there too.

The first dream was not really a dream. He climbed to the roof one night to look at the comet (the one named for the last living tiger). He'd put on his special hat. He was surprised to find his daughter asleep there on a carpet, with a bowl of fruit beside her and a candle that threw a dim circle of light that faded at the tips of her breasts, and the edge of the roof, and the lowest fronds of the date palm near. She was having a good dream; she was squeezing her mantle between her thighs; it was abundantly clear what was going on, for the smell of her rose-water filled the air, and up in the sky, where there should have been stars, there were a thousand small faces of men with dark curly hair and blue eyes, strangely alike to the face of this young man. (He pointed at me.) He watched her till the dream was done, and then climbed back down the ladder.

He took to napping in the afternoons. His daughter tended the shop. Sometimes he quietly pulled the curtain back, and watched her move about the small room, stretching (the lift of her breasts!) to finger the ceiling, bending to put her head through the window, gazing down the street: the camel, the jewels on the dome, the smile of the great-hatted goatboy. She smelled good; she had hips like a jar full of olives.

Once while he slept something warned him to awake. He looked out at the shop. She was talking to a strange young man, a foreigner. She was leaning nearly over the counter, her toes barely on the floor, her belly against the tabletop. That's what the stranger was looking at. She pointed behind her toward her father (as if he, too, were a jar). "To-night," she said, "when dreams brim his skull, come hold my hips, and kiss, the lips." The stranger went away.

Haroon didn't speak at once. Instead he lay back for a while and thought about what he could do. But while he was thinking, a deep sleep returned to him and he didn't awaken till the moon was high. "That was a bad dream," he told himself. But you know what he found when he lit the candle: his finest vessel gone, a piece of it on the floor.

He didn't undertake to follow her until much time had passed. He spent many days in his dream house, made a few small pots to keep alive, and spent the twilight hours in idle conversation with the goatboy, whom he sent to the market for wine and cheese. He told him everything he knew. Gradually the twenty-year wind cycle brought the sandstorm to his, the Eastern, quarter of the town, and no one came through that gate. All passage and all commerce took place at the Southern wall. So Haroon left his shop, just as it was, but for the shard of pottery (some stem and the leaf of the flower), which he put in his purse, and started for the Southern gate. The goatboy went with him. They stopped to buy provisions in the bazaar. While they waited for a caravan to join, they watched the flurry of activity in the center of the square. Some men were erecting a tall stone tower. "To watch the eclipse," they said.

The story of the travels of Haroon the Jar-Man and the goatboy, and of how, in a rainy village in Western Scotland, Haroon was bewitched by a warlock with an evil walking stick ("a piece of the Tree of Life"), whose image drove out all of his other memories, so dear and well-designed, and of how the goatboy came to lead Haroon across the great water, is a much longer story than this, and I'll tell it in the days to follow. It is said, and rightly so, that we never really forget anything. But for now I won't remember more. (So the old man ended.)

And it was true. He dangled the jewel. There was nothing in it. The sunlight shone through it, and some bounced away. Then the jewel itself disappeared.

"Let it be," he said (almost as if a question).

"Let it be," we answered, sitting back.

Not much time passed before I went outside. This is what I saw there: my father had sat himself down on one of the campfire stumps, and had taken off his sneakers and put them on another stump. He was slipping his feet into a brand new pair of leather boots. They came to the middle of his shins. I rubbed fingers on them.

"Those are beautiful boots," I said to him.

"They are, aren't they?" he said. "Mark just came up from the Plowshare to give them to me. He made them himself. He said he thought I'd need them soon."

Both of us wondered what Mark had meant. We rubbed our chins. He was usually right about that sort of thing. I looked down the meadow and could just see him disappearing into the woods near the cemetery. He waved and called something out to me, but I couldn't understand. There was someone waiting for him under a tree.

My father liked the boots. "Now I've got a pair like yours," he said. They made him feel like dancing. He stood on the stump and tried some steps, and then he jumped to the next stump and tried a few more.

"There's your saber saw," he said, pointing to the third stump, "I took it out." He handed it to me. It was a present from Kathy.

We went to the outhouse. He held the door open to give me light, and I sawed the second hole till it was about the same size as the first. The pieces fell down into the shit. Then we stood a while in front of the door. It has a little window shaped like a rose.

Verandah was leading the old man to where he

" THOSE ARE BEAUTIFUL BOOTS," I SAID TO HIM.

could get some rest, down where she sleeps, in the old chicken house ("The Sleazy Pines," she calls it). He waved to me as they turned the corner of the house.

"Good luck to you," he called.

My father and I both waved. We liked him a lot. Rosemary, the goat, came round the house just then, and the old man stopped to speak to her. I didn't hear what he said. She took a little bite from his loincloth.

"It sounds like he's got a good story to tell," I said.

"It sure does," my father said. "Probably has just about everything in it."

We were quiet for a while. Then he spoke again.

"It's a shame you won't be here to hear the rest of it."

That didn't upset me. I didn't think I'd be gone very long. "You can tell me the whole story when I come back," I said.

He didn't answer. He just looked down, and said something else instead.

"Will you do me another favor?" (I nodded.) "When you find your words, and you bring them back home, would you write this all down?"

I said I would. "It's the first thing I'll do."

He was happy about that. He squeezed my arm. "You'd better go pack your things," he said.

T here's not much to pack—things you'd expect, so I think I'll just write about Lila instead, 'cause she's right behind me, following me up the stairs to my room, her hand in the back of my overalls, her grin when I look behind; I've wanted to make words about her since I first opened my eyes at Spirit Lake, and found her sitting on the log beside me.

Her hair is the color of hay in the barn, and her belly is as soft as a salamander's throat. All her dresses are full of holes. She likes to rub her cheek on anything smooth. Her father works part-time at the mill. ("The place full of toilet paper down by the river," she calls it.) I can be standing with her when people have gone to sleep; we're warming our hands above the stove between us; the only sound is the hiss of the wood and her foot sometimes scuffing: we watch each other's eyes and lips and just when I think she's going to say something that will make the stove, the room, the house, and the mountain fall away, and we'll awake and surface in a green pool with a still sun and a cloud of hummingbirds above, she says instead, "I have to go get some wood." She'll disappear for an hour, I don't know where, and the stove comes cool to the touch. I forget how I pass the time. When she comes back she'll have three little pieces of wood in her hand, not even enough to toast a marshmallow, but when she throws them in the stove somehow it sighs and creaks and blazes, hot again for a couple of hours. We stand and warm hands as before.

I can't always tell her apart from my favorite image of her: I'm sitting in the chicken room, down in the bottom of the barn, on one of the overturned buckets, serenading the ladies (so they'll lay more eggs), playing "Annie's Lover" on my C Harmonica, when Lila comes in, swings the door shut so Rosemary can't follow: one great squawk runs the length of the chickens and Tidewater, the rooster, flies at her and then thinks better of it, landing at her feet. She's got her gray dress with the flowers on, over her dungarees. Especially when she sits on the bucket near me, the hens gather round her: they seem to be able to follow her thoughts, sometimes all quiet, watching her from corners of eyes, then all of a sudden clucking and flying away. She sits there a long while, then she kisses my shoulder and leaves; she pauses a moment before the framed picture of the White Mountain Leghorn up on the wall (staring down like one of our Puritan ancestors), the glistening red comb, the reptile eyes, claws deep in unstained sawdust. I put my harmonica to my mouth again, wait for a tune:

This is what comes. It's called "The Skin River Blues."

This sort of thing might have happened at sunset, but it didn't; the sun had just gone into decline, when Lila looked down from my window and said (her lips on the grain of the casement),

"They're getting ready to go."

And so,

I went to see; I stood behind her back, leaned against her, my one lump between her two, chin down her shoulder, but I didn't see exactly what she saw (my father, the train man, the Do-Nut truck, the crowd); I saw what I saw from the chicken-house window, that day:

My left hand on the broom, harmonica in my mouth, the haydust settles where she's closed the door; running footfalls, then she comes into view: she and her breasts go bounding up the hill. It's maple-sap time. She's running up to the Sugarbush to stroke the trees.

Who ever thought
To hang those silver buckets
There?

(Dale and Ray have lugged an old stove from the barn and built a fire. The sap steaming there. Dale mixing pancake batter. Ray takes his shirt off; the first time since October.)

I want to sweep the chicken house, or I would follow Lila up the hill, in one of the ways I know how: grab the rooster Tidewater by the tail, say a spell; he becomes a great stone peacock, richly carved, and I ride him uphill to Lila, the peacock flying free from the stone. A word freed from the chest to become a story that everyone knows. As we fly I hold his neck and he sings me a song. The first note like a dungeon door swinging shut.

We alight beside her, sitting in the peach-mud, melting bottom snow runs down her legs. She won't look at me, but she'll take my hand, she won't look away from the foot of the hill.

It's too sad to say, too sad, what she sees there: the wasted plain dry as a broom, the great log-filled gashes left by the torrent, the rock falls, the smolder-ing shells of rooms, the dark men working nervously on the temple, glancing now and again at the ocean straining toward them. I let her know with my hand: if there were some place I could take her—

She seems to understand, and it's enough. Things could be worse. She could be a stone, running down-hill on the water. She could be the water. This is what she whispers to me:

Our home lies
within the land
of which
your soul sings

What she whispers is one half of a circle. The other half is what I tell her in return:

"Singing makes it so."

We go down. The circle stays there, floating above the old weeds and the run-off, pulsing; Ray and Dale are watching it, hands over eyes, when we join them at the bottom. We stick our faces in the sap steam, Lila's hand on me, low. Ray talks about what birds have come back today, what relics of the summer the melting snow's revealed. (He doesn't mention the circle; it's just about gone.) The first day of spring. The mist on the greenhouse glass. Ray squats before the stove, feeding it branches, chanting an important mantra he's just made up:

> *Equinox*
> *sticks in box*
> *no more wind,*
> *no more cold*
> *nice*
> *big*
> *dog*

Then none of us speaks again. We just stand around the stove, feeling like quiet trees in the Hardwood, beneath whom a girl is asleep. One proceeds with caution, the first days of spring. We heat up some milk for chocolate, up on the butt end of the short stovepipe, an afterthought. Hold out our cups, a quick gust of wind while it's poured, in my hand the harmonica dripping with milk. That's the last wind I remember of that winter.

I'd follow her uphill, and so, and take her down, but I want to sweep the chicken house. I watch her zig-zag till she's gone into the Sugarbush, and then I work: the soiled hay, the sawdust, chicken shit, feathers, and dirt, I sweep into a pile near the barnyard door. (We once ran a truck on chicken shit. It wasn't a bad idea.) The hens on guard in the corner. I open the door and send it all out: most doesn't go very far, to ruts and the shelter of stones, but the feathers, the black feathers, sail a long way: some catch and flap against the chicken wire, and some make it through, run downwind, long skips on the crust of the snow.

I'm looking out the window, pressed very tight to Lila.

"They're getting ready to go," she says.

It's true. My father waves up at me.

"Time to go!" he calls. A big smile. "It isn't spring!" He makes the sign of the burnt toast, forefingers and thumbs framing his smile.

I wave back. I'd forgotten again.

"I'm on my way!"

A re you cold?" Silent asks.

Intermission
(Silent and
the Listener
in the
Graveyard)

"No—I don't think so."

The shiver in the dark. Another.

"Just a chill. It's gone now."

"There's no reason to be cold," Silent says. "Come closer." He offers part of his cloak. Unwrapping it slowly. The inside black as char, but flecked with minute points of light ("windows," he calls them) that you might have thought snagged on the billowing wool when he ran through a field of moments. In the sun. And the black-and-white dog at his heels.

There's plenty of room inside this.

"Warmer now?"

"Yes."

"What was I saying?"

"You waved back. You'd forgotten. You're on your way."

"Ahh."

Breathing of backs against the tombstone.

"I wasn't really going anywhere, you know. That was just the ritual."

"I thought it might be."

"The only time they ever use the train any more. Uncle John lives in the caboose. Used to take care of the train museum, he did. They left him one of their trains." A party of people from down at the Hollow on board that day, going to a reunion in the Northeast. The mayor rehearsing the speech he was going to give, after the fair, after the hike up the small mountain, the wedding of his daughter and one of their sons. And the mail. We all write a lot of letters. But for the rest: it was only a part of the show; one stop down the line I'd get off the train (maybe walk right back, home before dark, I didn't know); no need, on my quest for the burnt toast to move in space.

Must think about it a while. Up and piss in the leaves in the corner. Is that the face of a clown carved on the tombstone?

"I should have said so earlier. Before we made so much of the departure, and the time went so slow."

"That's okay. Taking little bites."

"That's because I didn't know how to say what happens next. If there will really be anything to tell. Did you feel that?"

"It was just a chill. It's gone now."

Sad blue eyes of Silent:

"I know, but if. If I were making all this up, it wouldn't have been a chill. It would have been four weeks of waiting. Walk in the woods. Bury beer cans, pick mushrooms. Build another closet in the room. Perhaps never tell another word. See only darkness. (My father was so poor they had to scrape the char off the toast if they burned it. And the cat waiting on the floor.) Sweep the hens again. Swim in the Beaver Pond. Meet a woman there. Slow forgetting. Forgetting is muscular. She'd touch me there—a little lower, no reason to tell any more of the story, or to save what's already been told. But it was just a chill, wasn't it?"

"Yes. I said."

"Let's walk up to the house now."

So out of the graveyard, to tea waiting in the house. They leave behind an offering, of piñon burning, and a handful of basil. The shelter of Silent's cloak as they walk, and the warm moon-gleam in his eyes.

"What's this place called?"

"My-Father-Lives-Here."

The sound of their slow steps as they come over the rise, duck the fence, walk up the path by the barn. Whinny of horses. The voice as they're lost in the shadow of the elm:

"Silent, I want you to know, anything you'd tell me I'd believe; that the sun sets in the East, that you've never spoken a word."

That's what he's wanted to hear. They sit a moment on the stone bench. Silent asks a question:

"Do you know a little bit more about the burnt toast?"

"Yes. A little bit."

Silent takes off his cloak in the Green Room, hangs it on the Duck Lamp. Raymond standing by the stove; nobody else around. He's holding a pot of coffee (Ray loves coffee), wearing his pink-lensed glasses, no other clothes but that.

"You have to be naked to write," he always says. Tonight he's writing letters. One to Alabama, where they make the stoves. Just to say hello. Another an answer to a matchbook cover: "Learn Re-Upholstering in Your Own Home." One to the Midwest, signing up for a Mail-Order Bride. Meet her at the train. A bouquet of carnations and a bottle of barley wine. Walk her slowly up the Old County Road, stopping many times to sit on the moss and make promises. There's many the star above, many the leaf below.

Sound of laughter from the bath. Silent warms tea. Smiling. Then rocking in the rocker.

"How's the writin' coming?" Ray wants to know.

"Not bad," Silent says, "I took a long walk. Sat up in the orchard all day. Then in the cemetery."

"Ah, the boneyard. That's good. You'll be able to finish now."

"I will, yes. It won't be long. It was good to know you were here all the time." Watching while all the passengers are asleep. His hand on the tiller. "I wasn't worried at all."

"Nothing to fear." Ray spits on the stove. "Though wind storm and rain blow." Making binoculars of his hands, putting out his chest. Sense that the house will stand a while more.

They stand at the window. Outside, the red barn shaped the special way you know now, with the shadow (in the moon) of elm branches there, many things sleeping inside. All about to disappear.

"Couldn't get more like it than that, could you, Silent?" Ray says.

"Nope. That's just about it."

"YOU HAVE TO BE NAKED TO WRITE," RAY ALWAYS SAYS.

Part 2

Don't Worry. Be happy.

—MEHER BABA

Does this path have a heart? All paths are the same: they lead nowhere. They are paths going through the bush, or into the bush. In my own life I could say I have traversed long, long paths, but I am not anywhere. My benefactor's question has meaning now. Does this path have a heart? If it does, the path is good; if it doesn't, it is of no use.

—THE TEACHINGS OF DON JUAN

I realize all the uncountable manifestations the thinking-mind invents to place wall of horror before its pure perfect realization that there is no wall and no horror just Transcendental Empty Kissable Milk Light. . . .

—JACK KEROUAC

Down in the bottom-land, next to the train, the four musicians are Mariachis now, weeping tears, playing on harps and marimba, "Adios Muchachos, Compañeros de mi Vida," song of a soldier going off to the Revolution:

> *Today my turn to say good-bye,*
> *I must go far from my good woman . . .*

My mother puts a basket in my hands.

"Fruits and nuts and cheese," she says, "and bread, and something warm to wear."

Uncle John warms up the engine, comes out wiping hands on overalls, the insignia on the bib, of a long-nosed oil can, dripping a drop of golden oil on a field of blue. He scans the sky behind the water tower.

"How do you like the clouds?" he says. "They were left over from Brig O' Doon." He lights a cigar.

"They look fine," I told him. "You all did a good job."

Children climbing all over the engine. The engine making concertina noise.

"How does it run?" I asked him (talking about the fuel).

He wouldn't answer. "It runs," he said.

One of the porters told me later: "Honey and vinegar," he said.

Then the crowd seemed to fall away, mostly, back in the shade of the station-house roof, and I stood with Lila and Kathy, my sister and mother and father, my grandmother to the side.

"Give 'em hell, son," she said.

We all put our heads together and stood swaying.

The musicians fell silent, but for the drone of the lowest gourd on the marimba, that echoed in my chest. I felt it there. Whispers behind me, of women handing cakes and bananas to people already on board, and of a few others, deciding to go along for the ride, of barking dogs, children flicking colored boomerangs, the click of the wireless, the station-master signaling, to the next stop on the line, that the train's about to leave.

Then I stopped hearing those sounds, just felt the heads and arms of the people closest to me: Lila and Kathy, who promised to come and help me if I wanted; my sister, who hoped to have a child soon; my mother, who made all our clothes; my father, in his new boots and his cowboy hat, who did the best he could, who was going to die before the next sun rose, whose eyes were an inch from mine, who said, "I'll see you soon."

And the next image is nearly the same, except that I'm gone from it, sitting in the dark green velvet seat by the window, the engine athrob so that the lampshades over the aisle slowly swing, all in the same arc; the faces are turned up to me, of the friends and cousins spread the length of the little platform, of the musicians playing, now, the hymn of departure, and, in the middle, the small group I've just left, still holding on to each other. Uncle John sounds the whistle; I can see the brief shadow of the steam fall on the water tower; my father separates himself from the group and approaches the train, as close as he can. He reaches into the pocket of his old lumberjack shirt and pulls out his red bandana (for wiping his nose or wrapping shiny stones in); he leans up to me, tiptoe, and wipes the window clean.

"You can see better now," he says.

Then the train pulls out slowly. The children galloping beside. I can see better now, and my father and I stare at each other, waving and smiling, till we make the first curve of the tracks, down past the semaphore, the hobos eating in a stand of yellow willows, one of them brewing coffee in an old can of Snap-E-Tom tomato juice.

And then I can't see him. I'm part of a moving train, and I see, on one side, the long-haired cows, and the great white dairy barn, and the mailboxes of all of us who live up the Old County Road, and the dirt path up to Stevie D's horse farm, and on the other side, the Eastern end of the lake, where a party of fishermen are napping on the shore till sunset, when the trout really jump, and where the crayfish-and-newt-filled streams come down from our mountain to fill the lake.

In such a way, the story tells, many years ago, the ancestor I most resemble, bid good-bye to his old life and his family, on some sand road in the desert, at the bank of a baked-dry river bed, where the scattered bones of hunters, fishers, and washerwomen waited for the flood to flash by once again, and the thin range cattle grazed on the sagebrush and the flowers of succulents, and the scorpions and rattlesnakes brooded in the dark cracks: my ancestor embraced them and ate the sacred food, and was borne away by his feet, across the plain of cactus—Saguaro and Cholla and Prickly-Pear, standing like silent well-wishers at the station while the wind hummed a farewell chorus in the comblike spines of the giant Organ Pipes, and he climbed up the canyon, leaving his clothes behind (they later were found in a mountain lion's lair),

reached the top, was visited there by the Restoring
Angel, in the form of a Harpy Eagle, and went down
the other side, so they say, never to be seen again in
human form.

All of his descendants, we liked to say, were animals or plants, or both, and the only human thing
about them was their name, and that name was all
they had to overcome.

I was told this tale, just as I've told it to you, but
like many other things it didn't sink in, it didn't become part of me till one day in the early summer,
when I stood in the middle of our stream deep in the
Hardwood, my toes curled in the smooth stones, and
before I started thinking about where I was, the sound
of the rushing water flowed through my head, from
ear to ear, as if I wasn't there, in the same way that, a
few feet below, the cool water itself ran through my
legs.

I know that after a long while letting that happen,
I heard the rustling of leaves, and looked to see someone retreat, who had been watching; I swung up into
a tree to see: it was my father dressed for fishing, a
few nice Eastern brook trout hanging from his shoulder, making his way back to the house.

I didn't think much about it; I was very young.

We hadn't gone but about a mile (I don't think
it was more), when I thought this thought: that my
quest had nothing to do with covering any distance
on the surface of space among the objects-of-sense
that are just obstacles to knowing, and to the acquisi-
tion of power; it wasn't information I was seeking,

but experience of what was on the other side of it, and any way it came to me would be all right, so I might as well get off the train as soon as I could; getting on board was just a symbol.

Not many more trees went by after that, before we came round the first big bend, crossed the trestle in the great meadow where my father once caught an old wall-eyed pike who'd wandered far from home, and just past the trestle, between two soft hills, we slid to a stop. (We'd been traveling very slowly, slower than a stream of maple syrup in the early morning.) I jumped off to see what was up. Passengers leaned from the windows.

Up at the locomotive, Uncle John was puzzled. He was scratching his head.

"Hit a goat," he said. "Walked right up to the cow-catcher, and bumped into us."

The goat was lying on the embankment, watching us, pink-eyed, the way goats do. He didn't seem to be hurt very bad.

Uncle John climbed back to the cabin, then down again. He'd fetched his red and yellow gris-gris stick, with a picture of St. Nicholas in a bulb on the top, and a decal that showed a fleet of sponge-fishing boats on a choppy sea, and the sun shining through the clouds upon a peaceful shore, and underneath, these words in white ink: "Souvenir of Tarpon Springs, Fla." He tapped all the wheels (there were a lot of them) with the wand, murmuring something I couldn't hear, and then put it up in the cabin again.

"Let's take him back to the goatherd," he said, picking up the goat, draping him round his neck like a scarf.

"What about the passengers?" I asked. Some of

them had alighted now, were sitting in the meadow peeling fruit, and some were heading back to the trestle with fishing gear. They seemed to have expected something like this.

"It's part of the ride," he said, and we went over the hill. Across the meadow. The gray rocks, the soft ground near the streams, the clumps of milkweed, and Japanese lanterns, and Queen Anne's Lace. Blue-bottle flies. When he grew tired I carried the goat, two hooves in each hand, his warm belly on the back of my neck, the still-hornless head, pink lips nibbling the "Union-Made" label on my clean overalls. Behind the third hillock a plume of smoke, the croft of the aged goatherd.

He was sitting on a stone before his house, a green sash round his forehead. He was whittling.

"Ahh," he said, "you've come." He was brewing some rose-hip tea, and three cups were set, and a plate of goat cheese, wet with whey, and wild raisins. He was smoking a pipeful that smelled like the pine forest where the wintergreen and ginseng grew, where I used to go catch salamanders after a rain.

He took the goat in his arms. He tugged the two tassels under its neck, and scratched its back for a while. The goat ran off to join the herd.

Uncle John said he was sorry. The goatherd waved his arms:

"That's okay, that's okay," he said, "it was meant to happen."

Then looking at me:

"How's Rosemary, Silent?"

"Just fine," I told him. "Everybody seems to get along with her pretty well."

He made a nice offer then. "When she comes into heat, bring her on over and we'll fix her up real good for you."

He pointed to the right. The big brown-and-white spotted billy in the fenced-in place.

We sat still then. The old man whittling, Uncle John fingering the long shepherd's crook, I looking past the goat pen, over the hill, to where the meadow climbed to the rocky mound that marked the beginning of a trail into the Hardwood. I asked where it led.

"Picks up the main trail to Adam's Ear," the goatherd said, "the one that starts up at your place."

I knew it well, at the other end; I'd often passed the fork when I'd hiked the main trail a little ways, evenings when one of our horses had jumped the fence, and gone over that Mountain in search of delight.

Uncle John went round to the back of the house to take a shit. The tea began to bubble. I took out my fruit and nuts, and spread them on the bandana. The old man put down his whittling for a moment and looked me over, passing without haste from my hair to the tip of my boots. It felt good. I had the feeling that he could not see very well, in fact, but had the clarity that comes of looking slowly. Then I poured the tea, and he whittled on, and Uncle John came back, and we ate and drank, even from the skin of fresh wine that hung on the door of the cottage. Then John stood and brushed crumbs from his lap.

"You'll stay here?" he asked.

I nodded. I'd decided to.

He gave me a big hug. The strongest shoulders in

the county. He could split the thickest hardwood rounds faster than my father and I and Luis, all three together, could do.

Before he left he said, "Ask the goatherd about the burnt toast. There's very little he doesn't know."

Then he started off. The old man gave him the shepherd's crook.

"I want you to have it," he said. He had plenty more.

We sat a long while and listened. The afternoon was so quiet we could make out the footsteps of Uncle John, first on the flat, then the soft ground by the stream, the stone steps over the water. The passengers laughing, getting back on the train. The whistle. The half-mile journey to the next station, Happy Camp, where the gem-stones come from. Music from a small brass band there. The game, I'd often heard of, that John and the station-master always play when he comes by. The station-master stands in the middle of the tracks and holds up the palm of his hand. The semaphore down.

"What you got in that train there, Mister," he hollers.

Uncle John leans out the window.

"I got all livestock, I got all livestock, I got alllll live stock!"

So the station-master lets him through.

"You go right on through," he says. And then when the engine gets up a little steam, and clears the station and the water tower, and the boxcars people live in down the way, traveling about three miles an hour, Uncle John leans out again and looks back and shouts,

"I fooled you, I fooled you, I got pig iron, I got pig iron, I got all pig iron!"

They've been doing that for as long as anybody can remember.

After the sounds of the train were gone, I turned to the goatherd and said,

"Uncle John says you may know something about the burnt toast."

He thought for quite a time, sucking on his pipe. Then he remembered something.

"Now that you mention it," he said, "when I was a boy, there was a young man who used to come around here in the fall sometimes, and tell us a story about burnt toast. I don't recollect the story, and I don't think it had an ending, but that may be 'cause I fell asleep. He had curly hair."

I waited for him to say more, but nothing came. I didn't know what to make of it. I watched a pair of mourning doves land and take a drink at the pool.

"What are you carving?" I asked him.

"It's for you," he said, and he showed me what he'd done so far. It was a goat-horn, with about an inch of the tip cut off. Where he'd cut it off, he'd bored a hole down the length of the horn, till he met up with where it was hollow inside. Then he'd dressed the outside till it was smooth, and put a tight brass ring around the stem. Now he was carving the cut-off tip into a conical mouthpiece. He ran a tiny hole through it, and fitted it over the end of the horn, and held it up to the sun. It was twice-curved, rippled in white and gray. He put it to his lips and blew.

All the goats stopped in their tracks. The mourning doves froze at the edge of the pool. I thought that the West wind itself had stormed down from the Mountain expressly to sound its one note in my head, and drive out all the noise already there, as when, in winter, when the flue's wide open, a wind may rush down the chimney and blow the fire out.

"That's so your folks up the Mountain will know that you're here," he said, and he gave me the horn. He tied it to a leather thong, and hung it round my neck. Slowly the silence returned. I knew how wild grasses feel, bent over by a gale, carefully straightening again when the tumult is passed.

He stood up and looked all around. Leaning on my shoulder.

"Did you know this place used to be a village?" he asked.

"No," I said. I didn't know. Then I saw it was true. The stones didn't lie at random. Memory symbols kept clean of weeds.

"That fountain was the center of the village square. Mornings, when I'd be leading the herd up to the upper meadow, I'd always wash my mouth out there. Fill up at the spout on this side and then walk around to the other, where the drain is, and spit out. The church was over there, and some houses."

I watched where he said. I thought I could see them pretty well, behind the emptiness. I wondered why he had told me.

"The reason is, those mornings after the young man told his story, I'd always wake up and see him walking away. When the sky was still red, and the trees were black." He pointed where. Up the meadow. To the goats by the tiny streams. The ruined stone mound at the edge of the Hardwood. I decided to go there. It wasn't very far, and I could sit on some moss just into the forest, and wait for whatever was bound to happen. So that's what I did, whistling (my father taught me to whistle), after the old goatherd and I embraced, and shared good words, and I thanked him, and we promised to meet again.

I found a nice place to sit, on a log surrounded by brakes and moss and some big orange mushrooms, next to a spring that bubbled up there to feed one of the main streams of the meadow just outside the trees —I had to look twice at the spring, because it seemed that the pile of rocks it burst from had been arranged in the shape of a dragon's head. But I guess not.

It was a quiet place, and good to sit there. In time I took out my harmonica and started to play "We'll All Go Together (To Pull Wild Mountain Thyme)," the best song I know. I always have to get up and walk around when I come to the lines:

> *I will twine the mountains high*
> *And the deep glen sae dreary*
> *And return with my spoils*
> *To the bower o' my dearie*
> *Will you go, lassie, go?*

And I was walking around, threading among the trees about the clearing, feeling the shiver on my neck, under the bandana, when the first thing that was bound to happen, did:

A man hove into view, coming down the trail that I was soon to follow, singing along with what I played, and he's the one person I'll describe to you, in

words: he was as tall as a horse, brown-bearded, with
thick hair down his shoulders, tied with a black velvet
band, a golden earring in one ear, and a shark's tooth
in the other, a red face, eyes of brown flecked with
gold, a neck like a tree, from which hung beads of
chestnuts, garlic, shells, and dried seed pods of the
prairie yucca, no shirt, but a jerkin made from scraps
of fur: red fox and raccoon, squirrel, and a little piece
of bear, and trousers, flared wide at the bottom, made,
in the same fashion, from scraps of leather and suede.
He smelled like a bullock in rut (I liked the smell),
because that's what came down the road behind him,
pulling his cart, full of fresh-cut hay, still green,
around which a cloud of flies and bees and leaf-hop-
pers bounced in time with the bouncing of the cart on
the stones. They all stopped at the spring beside me
to have a drink. Two sister dogs, Kali and Clam,
leaped out of the hay to water, and then disappeared
in the woods.

We sat down together on the log. He picked bits
of hay from his fur. He introduced himself, and then
I told him who I was.

"I've heard about you," he said. "I got some peyote
from Kamoo yesterday and he told me about you. It
sounds like you're on to something pretty good."

I said it looked to be. Everybody needed something.

"Does it look like a piece of meat," he asked,
"when you have your eyes closed?"

I said yes. Sometimes it did.

He rubbed his knuckles on his cheek. "That's what
mine looks like," he told me. "I think it's a memory
of something long ago. Nothing personal."

I thought about that. It made sense to me. What I
knew before there were all these things to see.

Then he asked something else. "Is it encouraging, as if each time you see it you learn a little more?"

And I allowed as how it was. I could see that the carter thought a lot like me. Perhaps because I made him up. The instant I thought that, he seemed about to vanish (as when you put your finger in a puddle where your face is), and I leaned forward, tensed. But he rescued himself; his stomach made a noise, and "How about if we have a salad?" he said, and I relaxed; "I picked up some vegetables down at the Exchange. All life is food."

He took a string bag down from the cart. There was lettuce and peppers and celery and sunflower seeds. He had a big wooden bowl. The rest of what I had I mixed in, and some cheese from the kind old goatherd. And gathered some mushrooms and wild onions from the stream. He broke a couple cloves of garlic from his necklace, in they went, and oil and lemon and salt. It looked like a pretty good salad.

"Wine?" he said. From a skin hung inside his vest.

I didn't mind if I did. Both of us grinning. I was sure, when the sun set that day, it wouldn't sink over the hill; it would come to rest right in my heart.

We ate the salad. The big ox-carter rocking back and forth on his bare feet. I could tell that he was chewing, taking food in, as a way of warming up, filling up to the very brim, before he let words loose from his chest, which is what I knew he'd sat down to do, and I ate with care to show I'd wait till he was ready.

"Strange thing happened to me last night," he began, when we had finished. Looking back up the trail. Rolling a cigarette.

An image came to my mind, of my father in the

redwoods, in the blue light, and the deer trying to make sense of the new night. I don't know why. Perhaps a scent of wild strawberries somewhere.

I looked in his face and shifted a little on the log. Letting him know I was listening.

He inhaled. He put the leftover leaves (his own mix) back in the pouch. A curl of smoke up into the autumn leaves.

"Will you put it in your story?" he asked, and I promised. No reason to leave anything out. A vision of me stirring a vast cauldron of soup, over a honking pit fire, with a long wooden spoon, a procession of villagers and people from the Hollow, arriving to throw things in.

The ox-carter's story I won't tell as he told it, because it wasn't long after he started speaking that he'd just about run out of words, and decided to act it out instead in mime and friezes, spinning sometimes like a dervish, there in the middle of the clearing where the moss was. To an audience of me, the two dogs (he'd whistled them back), the ox, to whom I had not yet been introduced, and one owl who leaned his head through a hole in the tree above us. The sun, if you've been wondering, was in decline.

I put my chin in my hand and studied how he moved, and didn't hesitate to join him in his dance, when I felt I could. The first thing I became was a fisherman, casting his nets on the waves under the moon, lips opening and closing, his very body silver scales, while the carter played a beautiful woman floating in the sky. It felt good to be dancing again: whenever I do, I forget that I've ever done anything but dance, and even more than that, on that night I felt that I was dancing on a narrow bridge of moss, light yellow-green in the void night, dancing to cross safely over from a place that was disappearing, as places do, carrying on my back the very best of what would soon be ashes, going to lay it gently down in the place where I am keeper. So I danced, a passing dance, and the carter too, till the story was over, and then some. That's what we're doing right now.

Here is what he said, but briefly. He spent his words on general things all of us know: all this is darkness, seeded with minute sources of light; men walk about below, and speak of the light in ways that reflect what's in men; and no word spoken then is either right or wrong (this works out in the end), because the lights bloom from nothing, on consciousness itself, as fruit grows on a tree. Whatever you want to see appears there. The image of men, floating over an ocean, going home, on rafts of words. Their favorite ones. Feeding some to the sharks. No two rafts the same.

I get up to dance. The carter saying, "Everything you'll ever know, is there inside." His hand on my chest. We circle the water; this is what we mime:

It was his anniversary, and he and his wife climbed the cliff over Spirit Lake (the long way round, behind), the same place where the lonely catamount comes out on the scree and hollers. They eat the cactus buttons. Not the best year, it's been. He leans near the edge, balanced, not well, on a cherry cane. Firelight and music drift up from the lake. Smell and the touch of the mist rising. The woman behind him, mysterious as what's down there. Ruler of the unconscious. The need to speak, and she just a long coat blowing in the gusts. When he speaks, his words vanish in the hollow of her hair like wind in the mouth of a cave. She goes home, and soon he follows, feeling better alone.

They live in a trailer across from the sawmill. (I know the place; it looks like a silver bullet. Cages all around, full of rabbits.) He finds her sitting on the stoop, washing her feet by candlelight. Smell of mold wine inside. They pretend he's a sailor, and she a woman of the night. She has a little roulette wheel (a dried pea and twenty numbers) and some flowers, and a bed and a chair and a book.

But inside happens what often happens (it's happened to me): she slides like a fish beneath him, hard to hold, though both wanting to; she deposits her eggs in the sheets and slides away to sleep in the weeds; her eyes still open, and he's left to spray what he has, at random, over them, and warm them with his belly.

He'd tried again to drive Mescalito as he drives his ox, and one can't. Now sleep's only for her, taking the blankets to her side. Hard to breathe in the little trailer; he goes out and climbs up on the roof. Lies down and sees this, what he wants to see:

Above the trees, over where the ponies are penned, where in two months the Northeaster will come down, raining sawdust and snow, a woman floating, that he can have. Asleep in the green hay of a cart, the ox nibbling beside the road. When he reaches her side already someone's there, inside her: an old astrologer from the West Coast, wearing a pointed hat, who pulls out and runs at the sight of a stranger. Then the carter makes love to her, his beads around her head, a feeling like strawberries, but he's only one of many: after him comes the fisherman (my arms full of netting), and the girl's father, and the moon for good measure. The carter is the only one who doesn't seem to understand (I know the feeling), and he stands off to the side, leaning on a branch of silver birch, the one thirst slaked but wondering, is that, just that, all there is? Is he still standing, up on the cliff, seeing what I see, holding Lila on my lap down below?

The moon takes him aside. Puts his arm around his shoulder. Like two friends meeting at a bar, one of them rich and one poor. "You ought to be asleep," he says, "forget what you've seen." He gives him the cart and the yearling ox. "Just props," he says, and calls some more words after him. The carter rides home. Even the gods are the radiance of our own souls. Now sitting at the edge of the spring, he recalls the last thing the moon said:

"Don't put this story to practical use."

The carter worried. "I haven't, have I, by telling it to you?"

I assure him he hasn't. "Just the opposite." In a useless story to be told to madmen.

That makes him happy. He looks around, the forest turning dark. "I guess I'll leave now," he says, "home before night." He hoped I'd find what I want, also, up the trail.

I said I thought I would. It didn't matter what.

We put our heads together. An image came into my mind, from somewhere, of a toast-shaped window in an adobe steeple, an Indian boy inside swinging on the bell ropes, his legs going high overhead. The ring of the bells and the blazing sun. His laugh even he can't hear. I guess the carter saw that, too.

"Bless me," he said, and I did, and he went away, leading his new ox, whose name was Bhu. The cart rattling on the stones, the two dogs nipping at the wheels. The smell of him on my arms.

When he was gone I stood and closed my eyes and listened to the ending day, for as long a time as it takes for a mouthful of the clear water to bubble up from the spring, whirl around the ferns and the rocks in the pool, run out of the woods by the ox dung and down the long meadow, wetting the hooves of the goats as it goes, flow into the great wooden barrel beside the goatherd's house, come out the pipe at the bottom, travel through the pipe to the near side of the old village fountain, out the drain at the other side, down the stone gutter past the ruins of the church, into the stream that runs under the railroad trestle, all the way to the river that empties in the sea. From where it babbles to where it's silent (lost in the one roar of the sea); here on the stones the water telling me: spring, stream, and river—I wear each form till I don't need it any more.

Now I felt the day turning cool, so I reached into my bag and pulled out what was there: my sunflower shirt. It has a story too. (Most everything you come upon has a story worth knowing.) This one is called "Uncle Charcoal."

Very early one morning, some Indian Summer, I awoke with a funny dream in my mind: I was standing on the compost heap, playing with my tape-measure yo-yo, while Verandah told me about her power vision, which had to do with two grasshoppers making love on a cherry tomato. Then she took me to her house to meet the spiders; they had strung their webs along the window sill, like a row of booths at a county fair, of pretty girls whose kiss you pay for—I awoke and found the day was meant for walking; a heavy mist had kept the frost away all night, and now the mist itself was nearly gone. So I climbed down and started to walk. Old Pal, the circus dog, came with me. I passed Chicken Corners on my way; my sister was there gathering feathers with her dog Flora (the Lily of the West), who had dozed off with her head on a big cucumber.

"Let's go visit Uncle Charcoal," my sister and I both said at once, and so we did. He lived far off, but not out of the question, and we could stop at the sawmill halfway there, and have some grilled cheese sandwiches and water, and talk with the men round the furnace. We hadn't seen Uncle Charcoal in a long while, and in the past no week had gone by without his coming up the hill with presents: charcoal toothpaste and charcoal pencils, black ink in a dirty sheep's horn, bags of black wool, smoked cheeses and chunks of incense, and charcoal for burning and dyeing, and grafting trees, and apples so black you'd never know if they were red or green—he himself, all covered with soot, would sit and talk with us in the Big Room; he couldn't sit still for long, but strode about the room and waved his arms, trying other chairs, his eyes and teeth all gleaming; when he was gone you could look around the room and tell where he'd been and where he hadn't, and my father would stand at the doorstep and watch him walk down the road (I'd peer from behind his hip) and he'd say,

"He is the last of the charcoal men."

Once, only once, we went to see where he lived; we rode partway there on the sap truck. I remember the sign at the bottom of the hill: "Rainbowater" (to the left) and "Uncle Charcoal" (straight ahead).

We came through the soot-covered trees. He lived in an abandoned potato mine, and made charcoal in the clearing. (Many times I have asked Luis, who knows such things, about that potato mine, and he always has a different answer. The last time I asked him I guess I was thinking out loud; I was cleaning a load of fish that someone had left on the Old County Road, and he and Verandah were beside me shelling beans. Verandah likes to shell beans because it's easy on the heart; it's no more than what it is: her long fingers, the pile of beans of many colors, the cast-off pods, the nibbling ducks—I was thinking of the potato mine, and asked Luis to explain. All he said was,

"People have forgotten the old ways.")

Uncle Charcoal waved hello. He left what he was doing and made tea. Lapsang Souchong. He lifted me up high. He gave me a piece of jade.

"Wipe it off when you get home," he said, "it's real pretty."

I didn't do well that day; I covered myself with charcoal dust and kicked over the spittoon (couldn't see it) and went swimming with his dog, Maxine, even though the weather was cold.

"You come again," he called, but somehow we never did. When we arrived home all the dogs were sitting in a row facing West, barking at the sky; the air grew heavy and we, wild inside, and soon a great thunderstorm struck. I watched it from the loft in the barn, right under where the sheets of rain came over the roof and whipped down toward the hollow. The silver maple went down that day. Uncle Charcoal came to see us every week for many years.

We wondered about him as we walked, my sister and I and the dogs, and it didn't seem so far this time. The signs on the post were different: "Rainbowater (dry)" and "French Girl's Wishing-Well" (straight ahead).

We came through the trees; rain had washed some soot away, and the smoking black mounds were gone from the clearing. The apples were bright golden on the boughs (that's why he brought them to us!), and the birds that frequent ashes had moved on. Off on a rise stood two black crosses: Uncle Charcoal and Maxine.

The front of the mine had been scrubbed clean, and there was an orange curtain across it, and green grass before. Two girls were sitting at a wooden table, right under the rusted pulleys of the old tramway. One of them sat on a bench, and the other on a stone near her feet. They waved hello to my sister and me.

The girl on the bench spoke first.

"My name is Undine," she said. "I wish you well." I could tell that she really did, too. Whenever anyone came round, she wished them well, and continued wishing long after they'd gone away. Whenever you needed to, you could think of her up there wishing you well.

She had lived there alone a while, and then a friend

came to stay with her. She'd only been there a few days, but already she'd found something good to say to us.

"My name is Tuula," she said, "and I have been waiting beyond the years."

So we felt quite at home, and stayed and talked all afternoon. We built a fire and sautéed some mushrooms (they had revived the mine, were growing mushrooms in the darkness there; they showed us around, with a birchbark torch).

At the back of the shaft was Uncle Charcoal's room. They'd left it just as it was. All covered with charcoal, even the insides of drawers and pillowcases and salt shakers, all black—except for one thing.

"He left this for you," Undine told us, and she took a package from the trunk under the bed. We unwrapped it right there in his room. Inside were two sunflower shirts, as yellow as the sun outside the mountain, and if you don't know what they are I'll tell you: you plant the seeds in the spring, after the last frost, harvest the petals in late summer to make the yellow dye, cut down the plants in October and spin the fibers of the stem to silken thread, and weave cloth and eat roasted sunflower seeds all winter long. Each shirt must be hundreds of flowers.

There was a note with the shirts that said,

"I do not kiss you but the heart is."

"This must have been Uncle Charcoal's," my sister said, "and this must have been his wife's." (We didn't know he'd had one.) And there was no charcoal on them, so we guessed they'd worn them in some other place; perhaps she died, and he climbed to the old potato mine and lived the long remainder of his life in black. And who wrote the note, that had no charcoal, and when was it put in the box?

We put our shirts on (bright! and so soft), and each time since, to wear the sunflower shirt is a very special thing.

My sister and I had a long walk home. They walked us down to the sign.

"I am glad you came," said Tuula. "I have been waiting."

"I wish you well," said Undine.

Slowly I opened eyes again; the sky was dark red through the trees. I raised my goat-horn to my mouth and blew. So loud that the pages fluttered in my hands.

The sound of running footsteps in the Hardwood. The feeling that I don't have to move; life will blow through me as through a hollow tube. Then a voice calls my name: Kathy's.

She runs up to me in the dark, and covers me with kisses.

"I'm glad he gave you the horn. So I could find you," she says.

On tiptoe. So that her arms are far around my neck. I wish I could tell you well enough. Kathy's the most beautiful woman I know.

For a moment a hesitation in me, and I wonder why. Is it because I think she wants to bring me back.

She seems to feel the question, and she shakes her head very hard against mine:

"To take you further. There's a special place."

I offer her my hand, she takes me by the arm. We go up the trail, a gentle slope. She knows her way well in the dark. (None of us are afraid of the dark, except on the ritual nights, when we're all afraid.)

Our feet make a sudden hollow sound. A little footbridge. Just on the other side she stops. Right beside, I can barely see, a stunted apple tree. You find them sometimes on trails in the woods, the fruit small and wormy, misshapen, but delicious; the deer eat the windfalls; the wood full of dark spots when you carve.

"Hang your horn here," she said, and I did, and she hung something too: an opal I gave her once, set in silver. Then we climbed down the bank of the creek below, and followed a path worn beside it. To where the path turned off into a gully, that seemed to lead into the depth of the Mountain. Wild drooping boughs that brushed my face. Beyond them a little clearing, a narrow waterfall into a pool, the run-off forming a brook that trickled back to the stream we'd just followed. A shadow in back of the pool, I thought a cavern.

She let my hand fall away.

"Let's build a fire," she said, and we did. In a few minutes light enough to see where we were, and her cheeks, her eyes that didn't move from mine.

I saw she had something on her mind then, to tell me, but I didn't ask; it would come, and this was nice until it did.

She welcomed the fire. "Will keep the insects away," she told me. The midges and gnats and no-see-ums. But I knew she'd wanted it for some other reason. Insects aren't real.

She dipped her finger in the water. Sparkle of firelight there. And held her finger up. The water seemed heavy along it like oil. She took off her clothes and climbed in, disappearing nearly, deep, up to the neck. Her face waiting for me. I removed mine, socks, shoes, overalls, bandana, left to heat by the fire, and stepped in toward her. The water strangely warm. All of us have a memory, one at least, of a pool of water much warmer than we'd thought it would be. I stood, and she came astride me, legs and arms around; neck hollow and armpits, I smelled how hard she'd been running through the woods to find me. Till I blew my horn, the breathfruit, the ancestor's sound. She rested on me, and I at rest; we didn't have to hold on tight; the warm water seemed to jell and fix us there. Our breathing the sole source of the swells in the pool. The moon came up.

Drying off by the fire. I carved her a comb, seven teeth, very quickly. That's an easy thing to carve. Then I stood behind and combed her long hair. The water collecting on her shoulders, to beads that ran down her breasts and slipped off at the nipples, rain from the leaves of a tree.

We sat facing. Her neck forward, head down to watch the beads fall on her thighs. Her folded hands, between her thighs, placed or fallen there like a funnel, for me, into her; I bent and kissed at the top, where her legs came together, touch on my lips like an opened peach. And we made love, on the ground by the fire. As slow as we could. We never had before, if you want. Her fingers sometimes touching my eyes.

The smell of the moss under her head.

The Mountain customs are old and mean well, but sometimes I wonder. Wouldn't I be as happy always like this. Would there be something more I want, from inside or from far from home, something I don't know yet, can't even say yet, but will want to try? Like my father opening his mouth to speak, then whistling instead. The horsemen outside the window. Does she know anything about it, she who hides very little, whose eyes are wet now, and I lying still inside her.

"Why can't it be?" I say aloud, neither happy nor sad, the first words I say to her in this whole story, and she shakes her head. Doesn't know exactly; they don't teach that; but there's a story she remembers—I sit up to hear it; we move closer to the fire and feed it, leaning on elbows, her eyes like almonds, her voice, now a voice I've been inside, tells me the story of the Juju-be Tree (from a book she read about the Gobi Desert, where at night wayfarers huddle under blankets and tell stories, and the great sand blizzards come and cover them forever).

It's very short (I didn't make it up):

A prince of the East (perhaps a Turk) lost his heart to a beautiful Circassian princess, and took her far from home. She went unwillingly. Although her rooms in his palace were fine, and she had the best food to eat, and date wine, and the perfumed hasheesh, still she longed for home. The prince commanded his prime minister, who had many powers, to do what he could, and the minister, after much meditation and consultation with the spirits in the resinous smoke, came up with an idea. He had the view from her window refashioned to resemble the view from her bedroom at home, even to the stream that flowed through the garden, the animals in the zoo, the mountains far in the distance, the certain color of the rain clouds that rarely came near.

The prince stood beside her.

How do you feel now? he asked.

The tears welled out of her eyes and ran down her ivory cheeks.

It's very beautiful, she said. It's very like my home, but I miss the sweet fragrance of the flowers of the Juju-be Tree.

So porters were sent, who returned in about a year with the desired cuttings. They took root and flourished in the garden just beneath her window, blossomed when the season came, and in time the princess grew happier and was pleased with the kindness of her husband.

But every time the Juju-be Tree blossomed, and the evening breeze carried the wished-for fragrance up to her nose, though she trembled with joy to smell it, still she must close her eyes and say, it's very like my home, and a picture like the one I've never yet found words for came to her mind, and she felt sad.

Kathy erect in moonlight; she had to leave. (That's one thing her story means.)

"You have to go down there," she told me, pointing to the cavern. I nodded my head; it wasn't for me to doubt; she knew about things like that. The High Priestess, connecting the father and the son. (No one knew what Kathy did, times when you walked past the chapel and heard her quietly singing inside.)

"Come with me," she said.

"Where?" said I. (I was supposed to.)

"Ah," she said. "Down the dark vistas of the reboantic Norns." And I went, though I didn't know why. I got dressed, (she didn't); she glanced a last time at the woods across the fire and led me down, far, but not too far, along a deep down-sloping tunnel, full of a gloomy light that I thought came from the moon still on her skin. There was a smell of swans. I felt hopeful; glad, too, to have her hand.

I made her stop a moment. To whisper something. (I don't like to do anything in a hurry.)

"I don't have any words for this," I told her. (I wanted her to know.)

She touched my cheek. Not to worry.

We came to the stopping place called "Keeping Still." A seat carved into the wall. A dark torch above, to light when I heard footsteps.

She stood before me, arms at her sides, face up to me. I touched my mouth to her forehead and then we hugged, happy with what had happened, and sad, too, for what she had not told me and I had not guessed; she touched my back so that it rested, quiet, and we closed our eyes, and then she vanished like a May fly, the slap of her bare feet in both directions—farther down the tunnel (where her two weird sisters lived) or back to the pool and the forest, I didn't see; it didn't matter, one way she went, the other her echo, form or name, and the dim light went with her. I sat down on the stone, that was shaped like me.

I won't say I was afraid, but I wonder. I didn't know what to look for, but there wouldn't be much to choose from, I knew. I took my harmonica out of my overalls and then I put it back again, not making a sound. The smell of Kathy clung to me.

Slowly I passed into a state of waking sleep, that men have sometimes told about in words that surprise them, the way I'd often float, a while ago, when my father would wake me before sunrise to go trout fishing, and before my mind was cleared of the dream we would lie down again, this time on the summer ground by the stream, while up in the pines the sun came to glitter in the dew—

With my eyes closed I seemed to see, as then, the light in the dew and the steaming rocks, and some of the images, variations of the one I told you about a long time back, and shapes among these, of people I knew had come this way before, when someone else sat on this stone: the fingers and calling throat of Orpheus, followed by a score of frightened colored birds who stopped and fretted and turned back here; wind-tossed Ulysses himself, who crouched before me like a buffalo, and let me touch his terrible bow; the goddess clad in overripened fruit and sterile blossoms gone brown, in dry leaves and the frosted grass and seeds in crusty pods, who must come down here every autumn, leaving the world to freeze. And many others who walked with calm and some, magicians, who skulked near the wall in great fear.

And then I did hear footsteps, slow, and looked toward the mouth of the cave. Struck a match and gave light to the torch. The sound of my heart beat in my head. Not easy to sit still on the seat. Trying to remember her fingers on my back, the safe shoulders of her, the breasts that spread against me.

The footsteps approach the outer reach of the light,

halt for a moment, puzzled—I half rise from the stone—and then come into view: the lumberjack shirt, the cap and the new leather boots, a whistle more like a sigh, my father.

I jump and run to meet him. I didn't expect to see him here. I call him by name. The name I have for him. My arm about to circle his neck. And then stop as he stands still, drifting back a little. Eyes blinking as if they had been shut. The tears rolling out of them. Down to the shifting boots on the floor. What Kathy had not told me.

I try to hold him (just to show: what?), but he won't, looks gently past me, down the tunnel—sense of a wind behind him that he's riding, and I in the way, and winter coming on; he wants to finish this. I draw to the side and he passes, the touch of his right hand to mine; his feet seem to leave the ground and one warm breath, the last one, whispers from his lips and hangs in the air about me, as from a dust-filled attic drawer, pulled open after years to find it empty.

I move to follow but he turns and stares. Lifts up his hand, slow as a cloud, to say: not the time for me, this time; don't push the river, it will flow by itself. He steps a little farther into the shadow and where he's been he leaves an image of light like a footprint running, of him dancing in the air, kicking up stars, his strong wrists crossed on his chest, his big ears, his eyes closed, the great going-home smile, his face bathed in sun (he *is* the sun), and the curls of his dark hair the tracks that wandering planets make, limbs of the stunted apple tree, twisted paths in the Hardwood I still have to travel for words, to be Silent, his son, keeping still on the Mountain, where this begins and ends.

The torch hisses out and his image settles to the ground like ashes. No father.

I climb to the mouth of the tunnel and try to sleep, gingerly, careful where I lay me down; October seems to want something more of me, when all I want to do is sleep now, or failing that, to let reason sleep, and run off to play with my shadow brothers in the green, or go from the world that has no name now, follow my father's dancing boots to where we think we will find music, stopping for ages (they make you wait) in the Land of the Crestfallen, to sit together on the gray rock and eat butterflies.

I try to sleep, wishing I hadn't been born a tree, food for the cottontail deer in the winter, wishing I were a cactus, born of a bootless and hatless seed, made fertile by a night-flying bee, blinking my eye once, sagely, in the time it takes a man to live and die, slowly swelling with the rare water, growing spines to hum and scratch the wind's back when it comes down south to rest.

Finally I sleep, where the coals we left glow by the still, dark pool, where the moths come and land by the watchful newts, and where the shape of the one heavenly fuck that hallows this story is still imprinted in the yellow moss.

I like to take walks in the morning, so that's what I did. (My dream had heard the news, had taken it well.) Washed my head in the waterfall and ate what was left of the cheese, and went from the clearing—to go home, late or soon, or pass through Adam's Ear; it didn't seem to matter much now, there won't be any adventures now: if I found what I was looking for or not, all the same; if I went back to the Mountain and sat on the stump and whittled, long enough, some peddler would trudge up the Old County Road and dump it right at my feet. Or Kathy would come up from rummaging under the barn. Something cupped in her hands.

"Smell this," she would say, and I would, and that would be that. Disappearing over the house, my empty overalls and shoes left at the stump. Kathy dancing for joy, putting my clothes away for the son inside her. Waiting for the chance to follow. Remembering, each time she set a table outside in summer and they buttered slices of bread. And certain songs on the harmonica. The wood carvings on the Green Room shelf.

I followed the creek back to the footbridge, reached the trail, hung the horn round my neck again (Kathy's opal gone), and walked, into the Hardwood deeper. Just to put a lot of trees between me and the cavern. To think as I walked (walking! thinking!) putting words between—

The Jackhammer

Of one October (they're all the same), walking in the Sugarbush with Ray. The morning spent picking pumpkins, burying another stretch of pipe from the spring, guy-wiring the stovepipes on the house, gathering ground nuts and mustard seeds. Now up in the woods above the orchard, sawing up an ash the storm brought down. A feeling of October. Michael had found Pepper that morning, leaning her head against the horse and crying, the goat stealing the oats, the four old withered broody hens flapping around her legs.

"I don't know why," she told him. October trying to sneak inside her body, like the cold dog-prick of the devil.

Ray and I walking in the maples. Off the trail. Coming out in a lower corner of the meadow, where we seldom go. The rusted cutter bar and disc, two old cars of weeds, rotten boards with hand-cut nails I pull out and use sometimes, the old shapes and tools of iron we try to figure out. Pieces of chairs to sit on. The dogs nosing under the leaves.

This time a heavy cylinder covered with dirt. Holding it on our laps. Something I've forgotten, or never knew.

"What is it?"

"It's a jackhammer," he says. Vision of tearing up sidewalks to bury machines. What for?

"I wonder how it got here."

Ray running fingers on the flaking steel. The hole where the hose attaches, that makes the noise. Did the man John Henry whipped toss it from the train when he rode back to town? Didn't the rain make the holes in the road? Ray quiet till the clouds come up like a city. A scene of fresh streets growing past the magnolias that used to mark the edge of town, and Ray sipping tea on the porch as the parasoled women stroll closer each night. Stopping to giggle by the iron railing around the hole, "Men Working," and the warning light's red flicker splashes on and off their waists. The breeze that showers magnolia blossoms on their arms, their thin sweaters, and carries the smell of them to Raymond's nose. Wondering if to-night there are fewer stars, or more.

"Love needs its tombs, too," he says.

Standing the jackhammer up in the dirt. The three dogs, and Silent, and Ray, sitting on the hill in October, after woodcutting, watching the sun go down.

W alking up the trail—none of these distances are long—I slowly came from the wild part of the Hardwood, to where there were more signs of the coming and going of men: rocks that were strewn in the woods like letters now started to arrange themselves in walls, and the wheel ruts grew deeper, and there were nut trees, butternut, walnut, and the tall hickory, and the maples now showed the small scars of sugaring-off. No down trees; people had dragged them away for fuel. Here and there signs of an orchard gone under, and boulders you could tell were for sitting, and paths that broke off to where men cleared homesteads, or came, time and again, to fish a certain pool of the stream. In such parts of the forest, midway between the settled and unsettled portions, men walking at night have sometimes chanced to see glowing gods nailed to the trees; we would feed a stranger at the farm and when the plates were cleared he'd lean back in the chair and tell us about it, while my father passed the pipe around and nodded his head. And if the stranger left I'd walk with him at least down to the forks, to try to learn some extra thing by being with him in the dark, and then hike home through the woods. Gods in pain I never saw or heard, but sometimes felt about to, and sometimes stepped on hollow-sounding places I never could find again in daylight; other nights heard an old tree creak in the wind and lit a match to find a name carved in the bark, or sat still and felt a hoot owl watch me, although I couldn't be sure. When I'd get back to the house my father would be reading *The Book of Lies* in the kerosene-lamp light; he'd lift his eyebrow toward me; I'd take out my apple walking-stick and carve another figure on it; one of the names my father had for me had something to do with this. Walking one sort of stranger back to the main road at night.

Thinking, walking, the sun just coming up, I looked over the rock wall and down the slope. A stand of trees in a little meadow. One of the trees was a girl, holding her hands above her head. I went to see. A great tree fallen across the path. I crawled under it, and when I stood and looked again she was gone. I walked to where she had been. The leaves greener there than elsewhere. There was a weathered sign on one of the trees:

FREE WORDS

and an arrow showing where.

It seemed like just the thing I was looking for, so I followed. Hoping the sign still led to something.

Through a hole in the thicket and over a rise; a fence, a gate, a field of late flowers and dung, a barn, a stable, a stream, and a girl (the same one) sitting under a shady tree. She smelled like milk. I tried to be matter-of-fact.

"Is this where the free words are?" I asked her.

She said yes.

"Yes."

"Wow, free words. That sounds like a pretty good deal."

"It's nothing to get excited about," she said. "Words are always free."

I thought I recognized her voice, so I leaned a little closer (pretending I was smelling the milk); I thought she was probably Lila, but I couldn't say. In this book Lila is the woman who wears masks and Kathy isn't (there's no reason; that's just how it is), and I try very hard to let that be. (Which is not to say that Kathy has no mystery; she has—secrets I'll never, or only accidentally, know, but always feel sure that they mean something good for me: that's how she is. I know for example that only last week Spirit Lake Fritz put his old black lunchpail under his arm and put on his gray felt hat and pretended he was going to work at the sawmill. He walked down the Old

County Road whistling "Follow the Drinkin' Gourd." But I know he turned up toward the Sugarbush and walked right through it, and didn't stop till he'd reached a special place, where Kathy was sitting down, between the waterfall and the old sawdust pit. She reached into her pocket and handed him a yellow fruit, and after a time they parted. All I know is what she wanted to tell me:

"Something happened a long time ago and now every autumn I must pay him a quince.")

All this has to be. Perhaps in some other story we would work this out some other way, but I don't know. Without traditions, whole families can become confused, and vanish as quickly as a plateful of pie. So I just leaned close, and didn't question.

"Would you like some milk?" she said.

I did, and offered my hand. Pulled her up and we went into the barn, to a cow the color of cinnamon. She sat on the little stool and fell to milking, with her cheek and part of her hair against the cow's belly, and her mouth slightly open. The milk started to squirt into the pail. The first sound it made as it struck the cold pail was just the sound you might hear if you were sitting on a cold mountain at sunrise, and far down in a valley you could hardly see, a church bell began to ring.

I just stood by her side. There's not much you want to do when you're watching a girl milk a cow, except stand there and fall in love, and watch her hands and warm your own hands in your pockets, and bend down and kiss the soft hair on the back of her neck, if you know her, and maybe walk around to the front and say something nice to the cow.

We carried the bucket outside. To where there was a cup hung on a tree. She dipped and filled it, and held it out to me.

"I'll be right back with the words," she said, and went out of sight, around the barn.

I sat on some grass, still wet with the dew, almost crystal enough to be frost. The ground a little harder each morning now. Orange of dawnlight in the bubbles on the milk—milk, warm on my hand and down my throat and down, milk that never had to be cold— I thought how just one (only one?) dawn ago the dogs and the goat raced up the hill and I sat in the outhouse with my father, as close as could be, and he looked through the hole in the wall. And now he would be spirit. I knew that much, that he would ask to be carried off on the wind, and not put in the ground, which was turning so cold. He always felt closer to air and fire, and even water, too, sometimes, than to the earth; you may have sensed this by now—

She had come back. Was sitting beside me and drinking some milk. The foam around her lips. Mist about her head. She was wearing a long gingham skirt and she had a brown wooden box in the dip between her thighs. I looked at her face and realized I had missed her while she was gone. I touched her knee and told her about my quest.

"Then don't look any further," she said. "I've got all the words you could possibly need. Right here in my lap."

I looked down.

"Would you show them to me?"

"Let's go for a walk first. I know a special place," she said, and she put the box under her arm and led me over the meadow.

"Would you like me to carry that box?"

"No, it's not very heavy."

We came to a stretch of rapids in the stream, and a mill built on the bank with a rolling water wheel, and over the mill a summer house with a striped canvas roof. We climbed up. The inside of the canvas was painted blue, with golden stars, and there were two colored-paper birds hanging down on strings, that flew around each other when the wind came through the lattice. The walls and the floor were painted deep red and there was a blue table in the middle where a candle in a glass bowl burned, and a circle of salt around that. All around the gazebo grew green willow trees. You always find them beside streams.

She put the box on the table and opened it a secret way. It was full of words.

"Take a handful," she said. "There's plenty. But put them back when you're finished with them. You probably know why."

So I reached in my hand and brought up a fistful. (That was then. Today I take them out one by one, and I pick them slowly, by how they feel.) I spread them out on the table.

There were words you'll easily recognize, like "Silent," and "ocean," and "Jubilee," and "beaver," "whistle," "stump," "suck," "silo," "tapping," "bittersweet," "catamount," "creeper," "hollow," "ear," and "Pie."

And down, potato, nozzle, clipper, rue, rising, penguin, hurry, marrow, mystery, snorting, hang, zoo, fog, along, love, jewel, woodpecker, sizes, peeled, balloon, dilate, purify, cactus, and name.

And words that fluttered in the wind that came through, catching my eye, beneath the slowly turning birds: scree, and silverling, stagecoach, newt, corn, mushroom, blow, trout, squawk, leghorn, gully, follow, sleep, toast, hunker, glowing, by, berry, later, wind, seasonal, tower, barn, and noon.

And words I've heard since, in stories, and may have a chance to use sometime (you never know), like oakum and wiggle and manse, and back-hoe, simoom, alder, wort, rennet, mortise, bedstraw, kore, colostrum, madroña, and tort, and dudgeon, and grume, and nutpick, amazon, pome, bucksaw, toponym, frizzling, and gat. And martingale, wood pussy, yaksha, yeti, kraken, pullulate, and rowan.

And some that I wrapped up, as soon as I came home, and mailed to a friend in town, as I would never (wouldn't want to) find a use for them here.

And some words, oppressive ones, that filled me with a fear I must have been born with, though the two-hearted men who fed on such fear are most of them gone or powerless.

And others I could barely make out, for so much light came through them, and others still, shy ones that stayed on the fringes, exiles, for some unmentionable reason out of favor: these I gathered in and mixed with the others; it's all the same.

(One of the signs we never painted on our barn says just that: "It's All the Same." Right underneath the two circular hexes I copied from a book of Pennsylvania Dutch design.)

The same, and the sun came higher, through the willow trees, and the words glowed where they lay;

the same, and a wind came over the meadow and brushed them: it might have blown them away and then, would I have stood or tripped, clumsy, in the summer house, like a dancer who hears, but doesn't understand, or would I have known, it's all the same ("He who knows doesn't say"), the words all temporary masks before the silence, each one my name for a moment before vanishing, the meaning not in the words but in the unfigured silence of the table they all lay on, the blue one, the black one, the colorless one into which the warm breath of the girl beside me (who smelled like milk, smelled good to me) fell, and disappeared, the girl who came very close to me, so that our hips touched and each felt something delightful there, as she gathered up the words and returned them to the box, and closed it in the secret way she knew.

Soon, leaning over the balcony, holding hands, looking down at the water. She can tell that something's not just right; up on the Mountain we don't learn to keep secrets very well.

"How do you feel," she says, and I still look down. The slow crank and turning of the water wheel, the second-best sound I know of; slow rocking of the whole building in time, and a broken window below, through which the smell of ground-up corn and rye, and birds flying in to feed there, swallows and mourning doves, nuthatch and woodthrush and wrens. And sometimes a silver fish swept against the wheel, and carried aloft in a pocket, and dropped back again into the millrace.

A feeling of always falling short, back where I came from: a touch, and no more, of the woman who's always a virgin. Will there be other chances. The only things new are the words (some very nice ones), and the softness and smell, and the rising, of these breasts near me, and now in my hands;

"I feel pretty good," I say. "I guess I've found what I was looking for." Picture of King Something discovering a few old oats in the bottom of the bag.

She looks in my eyes, no more secrets; we both know what I'm thinking. That I feel like the great warrior himself, suddenly coming to what seem to be his senses, in a lull of the battle, crying, what am I doing here, and casting his weapon away, till Krishna takes him aside and says, "These are only appearances, no more than objects of the senses; the warriors you slay have always been slain by you; wise men know that they cause nothing. Start thinking about something important," and then shows him what doesn't begin or end, what brings the soldiers, and generals and presidents, all to their knees.

She holds the word-box in both her hands.

"These are no good to you if you don't know what's behind them," she says, and it's true. And now eyes closed, facing the sun, the clearest semblance yet, of the burnt toast, my power vision. Knowing what is and isn't. Gaining power over words by visiting their source.

I wondered how. (But I really knew, already.)

She shrugged her shoulders. "If I knew," she said, "I'd write this story myself."

But she did. She knew as well as me.

"You may as well walk through Adam's Ear," she

said. Knowing that's where I was bound, when her sign led me from the trail.

Climbing down from the mill, dancing back up the meadow, stopping to drink more milk by the barn, but no hurry: so we spread golden honey on whole-wheat-and-rye bread, the cow watching from her window. We chewed, and it seemed that the honey, the bread, and the milk would never diminish if we sat and fed all day, and all night too, and more. Could learn as much, perhaps, if I stayed to do that, sitting under the shady tree, and she playing the old hymn on her Autoharp, and a year-long procession of friends in overalls and strangers coming over the fence and kneeling down to eat, all sharing, and passing on with smiles, as blood passes through the heart, and the cow and the horse, and the chickens, goats, pigs, ducks, and geese, all coming round with their voices, all, singing what I've wanted to sing all along: food, honey and bread, vegetables, milk, and grain, food; exhaling and inhaling, food; death and life, both food; growing old and begetting, food; feeding, and feeding-on everything, food; mouths sucking and kissing and praying, food; bodies filling and emptying, food; making the suns to glow, all food: so I've heard, to the tune sent forth in the morning calm by the barn full of yellow hay, by the trees drinking up cold water, by the birds flying back and forth from the mill, by the stream and the water wheel turning, by the animals down at the compost heap and the wild ones calling in the woods, the rats, possums, bobcats, coons, and bear, and rabbits and deer, and porcupines, foxes, squirrels, and skunks, and pickerel, pike, bream, carp, and trout, by her pink fingers on the strings of the harp, by my lips thick with honey on my C harmonica (a brand new one, like a fresh mouth to kiss), by these very words—then in the silence surrounding all this, while the food becomes us, so I've heard.

Yet I will go on my way—it's part of the structure, my birth and my name—and she'll carry the box of words to the farmhouse on the Mountain where my father once lived, where they'll stay, till I come back to tell this story with them, if ever I do, for it is said, and not without reason, that no man who walks through Adam's Ear can ever return.

███████████

"Some do."

The
Story of
Adam's
Ear

I rubbed my chin. I'd heard that nobody did.

"Yep, some do," the old farmer said. Sitting on a stump, blowing his pipe clean and then packing it tight with kinnikinnic. A cloud of yellow smoke. The kind of old farmer who's lived through so many hard winters and lean summers you could slice into his arm and read his story in the annual rings. He went on:

"Been sittin' here every day for thirty years, and I've seen people goin' both ways."

"But did they really go through Adam's Ear," I asked him. (I wanted to know.)

"It doesn't matter if they went up Jumbo's bum," he said, "it's only a story." That was true. As the song says, it all goes down to the sea.

I stood with him a little while longer, but it was clear he didn't have more to say.

"Well, I'll see you, then," I told him.

"Prob'ly," he said, and spat some juice on the fallen leaves. And I walked farther up the trail, the short way to where it met the main trail, and turned to the left without lingering, and went on. All the way to Adam's Ear (not very far). What little more I knew I'll gladly tell you, and I'll try to make it short (you'll see why):

Many people believe, and they don't mind saying, that life is a dream. My father was one of them, I think; he wore that button on his hat I've told you about already. But he never told me so in words; he wanted me to make up my own mind about it, and I'll do the same for you.

There was one person, though, a balmy historian whose name is lost (or may as well be) who lived, the story tells, right on our farm, a long time ago, in a room above the old tractor shed that blew down in the big wind in the time when the Two were One. His words never left the Mountain; I found some in the attic (no great surprise; they'd been found before) that said something like this:

He was thinking about his craft, writing history; it seemed ceremonial to him, like waking from the collective dream to tell it over. So sometime people would remember. But there must have been a time when memory and forgetting were the same, and both the same as experience. That was a good time. When did it change? Perhaps when man first decided he could cause change, could impress himself (and add something) to what seemed to be real. The first time this happened was when Adam bore Eve out of his own chest. So the first creative act of man happened while he was asleep. And every act of work or creation, from the first up to the writing of this line (he said), comes from that first division, and there's no way of telling whether he ever woke up. All this could be a dream of Adam. And there will be others.

He didn't write more about it, but the story tells that a long time later he awoke one summer morning (I guess he had had a dream) and decided, that if all this were in Adam's head, there must be some way out, a place you could step through and never come back. He predicted the existence of such a place, and called it Adam's Ear. (I don't know why.) And because he was old, and didn't care to walk far, he said it was right over the Mountain.

"Might as well have it close to home," he said. "No use havin' it too far down the road."

That very day (it wasn't even noon) he went over the Mountain and was never seen again. And the legend, as legends do, sends some people out that way, and keeps a lot of other people at home. So it all works out. I myself had been halfway there many times before this, once a month from spring to fall, when one of our horses would come into heat, and bolt, and run over the hill to Stevie D's horse farm, and I'd have to go fetch her, North, on the trail toward Adam's Ear. I'd turn off where the tracks of the horse turned off, down a stream bed that went right, and was soon lost in the trees.

I walked along slowly (not wanting to miss it), till I knew I was nearly there, a feeling like a wind I couldn't hear, always blowing away from me no matter where I turned, that carried off the sound of each breath as I breathed it, like smoke from sacrificial meat. No hurry, so I sat on a rock for a moment, and while I sat I composed a poem. You could hike up there yourself and see it, right near where the wild grapevine makes an arch above the trail, but I may as well leave it here, too.

Walking to
"You-Can't-Come-Back,"
I stopped to hear
wild goose wings
one last time

And walking, and sitting, and walking again, I met nobody, no one I can recall, coming or going—but when I tell this story again, it won't be like this at all, I know. Walking the same path twice, you can't help but find it different: some other time, coming round the last bend, I'll chance upon some shadow, a shuffling hour, or a fleet-footed minute, who, seeing me, has just enough time to adjust his mask and put some shape on, or pass for a tree, before we pass each other on the trail and tip caps, or stop to exchange light words, as wayfarers do (it could happen; days and nights are travelers of eternity, poets say).

The first time it may be Sam, just back from growing lettuce on the coast, a big clean stick in his hand and the sun in his red beard, his pockets full of pure rock candy and fresh lemons, the dungarees that smell like motorcycle; we burst toward each other and go through the ritual of greeting:

"Sam, you old lettuce-head, you!"

"Silent, you old tumbleweed!"

Then he'll sit on a hunk of crystal and wait while I walk through, where he's just come. (Takes only a minute.) "You'll feel like a new man," he says, "and then let's go to the Amazon."

And the next time I tell it, I'll meet Kamoo, walking as slowly as any man can, leading his turtle named Taj on a leash. Kamoo's a master of the turtle oracle, of which I can't say more. Kamoo eating a candy bar. A Sky-Bar. Big enough to share with me. They have them in the machine down where he works.

"Long lunch hour today," he explains, "so I decided to take young Taj here through Adam's Ear."

I stroke the turtle under the chin. He can't complain.

Then Kamoo hunkers down and motions for me to do the same. We're facing each other.

"Lean your head back," he says, "and I'll blow some of this dust up your nose. You'll feel like ten circuses, I guarantee."

So I do, and he takes out his pocket-size porcelain mortar and pestle, and crushes a piece of some South American bark, puts it in one end of his blow-pipe (an old plastic pea-shooter, striped red and yellow), puts the other end up my nose, and blows, and laughs, and then goes dancing down the trail, high-stepping now, the turtle Taj under his arm, and I go on to Adam's Ear, sitting right there in the middle of the trail.

Sometime I'll tell it stranger still: just about to step through (thinking, who is this stepping this step?), I turn and see a movement through the trees, a flash of color and another near it: I wade through the bramble to a stand of oak, parting the moss with my hand and the rare mistletoe—a low moan from the shadows, and from me; two women I know on a bed of herbs, one dressed like a dove and the other a serpent so green, feather and scale coiled in one and the sun pulsing down, songbirds confused in the limbs above. The two can't see me, and I can't move away, because I'm caught inside their kiss.

Or I halt as I step on the threshold, and then don't believe any more; I turn and run back down the trail, past the two spurs you've heard about, over the Mountain and down the other side, never stopping till I've reached the crossroad, the wayside altar, and just beyond, the brown house, the farm where the women chop wood well and we all gather pumpkins and corn, and sometimes we feed each other with our fingers, and make music and tell the old stories, and you can sit in the outhouse with your friend or your father, and look through the crack and see yourself die: Rosemary the goat and the new charcoal puppy, Katy Crewl (The Roving Jewel), and the horses are all standing round the salt lick, licking, and Michael and Raymond look up from haying,

"Silent's come back. We can all breathe a little easier now."

And Verandah comes out with a bucket of cider.

"Well, did you find Adam's Ear?"

I shake my head between swallows. And golden juice dripping from the hair above my eyes.

"There's no such place. It's just a story." Wiping my mouth on my arm. Jumping the little stone wall, to go sit and swing in the tire. Wondering if I'll ever see the burnt toast again. And seeing it right then, with joy (that I may learn a little more about it). Always the same face toward me, like a teasing dancing girl, never quite showing what's behind. (Nothing to show.) A voice from the raspberries says,

"I become aware of something in me which flashes

upon my reason. I perceive of it that it is something, but what it is I cannot perceive. Only meseems that, could I conceive it, I should comprehend all truth."

It's Luis, coming out of the bushes, in the white robe, berry-stained, that can't hide the smell of cow dung and our best applejack; he tosses the book to the grass and comes to swing me, higher and higher, singing a song of no matter, higher,

"Look around you," he calls, and I seem, at the top of my swing, to pass through a window of red autumn leaves and dream, while I hang there, a round place of man-sized fruit and bursting flowers and mirrors that vanish and silence, walking on ground made of cobwebs that nearly give way, all colors memories of yellow; a boat slips by, on a canal filled with feathers, Kathy paddling with her hand, Richard in the bow, both smiling.

"Why are you telling this, Silent," he wants to know.

And I go off and put my chin in my hand. They keep slipping by, waving every time (the canal just goes round and round). Each time an old gander walks out from behind a tree and sighs, and then goes back to gather his voice again.

I'm finished thinking. "So the story can say, 'I'm being told,'" I answer. Myths where there were none, or some nearly lost. That's the right answer (but I don't remember why), and they paddle away.

Or: I'm still sitting on the orchard hill, haven't moved since I returned from the banks of the moon. Finally (How can I possibly tell it? To tell it is to come back empty-handed), I forget why I came to sit here, forget that my eyes are closed, that I'm not a stone or a divot of dirt and straw, that the quiet breathing is mine (not mine!); this is a ferry I'm on, but I forget where we pushed off from, and don't know where we're going, I don't know, but it's bound to be good. I don't know, but there's room—

There's room, room, my overalls have plenty of pockets; I'll put all these variations of the story in pockets all over me, stuffed in with what's come before, and there's more room still, for anyone that wants, for anyone that came down off the Old County Road to sit and listen (this is why you didn't pass by), still more room, for things you want to bring along or tell me, recipes, mantras, adventures, friends of friends, someone I may marry, children not born yet, photographs, pressed flowers and leaves, standing stones, farmhouses built on the ashes of older ones, bone dust, natural sounds, music, dances, words (from the word-box), and news, only good news, and love— room for anything; I grow lighter with each addition; it's out of my hands now, and I've only one more thing to tell before we go home, once before time comes to cover it: the truth, just how it was, going through Adam's Ear, because, I've heard it said, a few true words have enough power even to topple oppressive governments (so I've heard); so pass on these: circles and space, touching hands, my father's whistle, water flowing strong in all six seasons, the Hardwood larger than measure, going home, round canals full of feathers; only unreal things begin and end,

It's true.

And this, too:

That where I was standing was Adam's Ear.

That I sat and hummed. I did the hum called "Clouds Disperse," and then I stepped through.

I want (I really do) to make this as short as I can, because I'm anxious to bring us all back home now, and because it just wouldn't do to try to explain what's better left as a story, and that made of simples, just as it wouldn't do to spend time looking back; how we came here isn't important.

I walked through, it's true, and didn't fall from anywhere; nothing at all seemed transformed or annihilated, among the objects I'd come to love in the world the eye can see, the plants and stones and birds whose names I knew. And I didn't spend much time on the far side of Adam's Ear, it's true, and didn't walk further afield, as many since and before me (all of the vanished ones) certainly did—it was clear to me that just like other stories (we just happen to inhabit this one), and riddles, charms, and devices without number, the legend of the dream, and of the door you can't return through, is what you make of it, whatever your own quest has to do with, and I wanted to go back home; my father was dead and I'd found some words, so I just turned around and stepped back through, on my way home, not doubting that I could, as though I had looked up from playing in the yard, and smelled some fricassee just out of the oven, the sun descending, orange in the kitchen where my mother stood by the Home Comfort stove, and the friends in the meadow laying down hay rake and hoe.

That's when it was, when I stepped back through, that the most that was ever meant to happen in this story, did; all the loose but beloved structures were lost for a moment in the one thing that surpasses them; it's true, I was there (more or less), and since then, at least, I've carried Silent, my name, slung over my shoulder wherever I go, and I like to sit like this, slowly down on stumps, on yellow humps of moss, on headstones, porch swings, pumpkins, laps, sap buckets, rafts, and wells, and tell all passers-by: this world that was born in silence is returning there, I know, and that's my story, and it too would be perfectly silent (and will be, there's time), but that I thought it would be fun to tell it.

And ask me nearly anything at all, ask me what week in April the spring peepers awaken, or how the newts feel, molting in the new green ferns; ask me the sound of a tree full of blackbirds, or how to make a goat-horn, or how to track bees to find wild honey (you need flour, and sugar water), or when to plant cosmos or pole beans or thyme, or what herbs to boil in the sauna, or how to bake a chili pie; ask me why rain and fog make me warm all through, and why all the dogs on our farm roll on their backs and open hind legs whenever any of us come near, and why I think I could stand here and knead this soft loaf of bread all day, ask away, but don't ask me to tell you, in any way but with an emblem or two (and I'll be glad to), what I saw when I stepped through.

I no longer have any doubts, or many, that we're together now, not to say much more than needs to be said, and not to wonder why any of this is: it has to be; it all has to be.

We've spent a long time (not much longer now) in space between, like a dark room we entered from different doors, and sat quite still in, while slowly it grew light. And vegetables, and women, friends, words, the burnt toast, and my father danced through, the dance of aboutness, trying on faces and casting them away, always about to tell, but never quite, what remains when the last surface is gone, what's left of the corn in kernel when the hull and the grit are gone.

When I consider the toast, I think especially of the two women (both mysteries to me: a mystery, even, what we can do together), and now of the third, for there is one, in a way—we need names for things we think of, and when I think of the toast as the wall, always dissolving, between me and the emptiness, the only thing that's real, when I think about it, I always come again to a woman I can't see, who, lives, perhaps, in the forest, and is the forest, and more: who's beckoned to me since I was born, and also let me know, in ways that could have made me happy or sad, that, she's been here inside me all the time—

Let it be: Silent, I, in overalls, mountain boots, and the red bandana, inside of whom words have rattled life-long, like seeds in a dried gourd, and in whom the walled soliloquy that separates our minds from each other, took a visible, accidental form that just offered to be pierced, with a cry of awakening (I am!) and delight (I am not!), stepping through a place called Adam's Ear—there are more places like it than there are trees in the Hardwood—with an offering of the best I have, cupped in my hands; for a moment that might have been days, the trees and the rocks, and the birds, clouds, hills, and the trail seemed all to vanish into an emptiness I knew I knew, and I, waking from a dream in a room perfectly dark and embracing, filled up with love and did the only thing I could then: let my hands fall open and the seeds, words, I was holding there, whirled away into the dark, and flickered on and off like fireflies, as we do, silent and glowing and temporary, forms that thought puts on for a moment, all of us metaphors for the void (and nearly knowing so, sometimes), welling up from, falling back to, what never changes, nothing, all the same, okay.

All the old illusions came back soon (they do when they hear you talking about their absence), and the Hardwood stood just as it had stood, and I somewhere in the center, but that was okay too; I knew I was bound to forget again; there would always be that, as I grew older.

I wouldn't want this to be any other way (and I won't leave till it's time), but there is one thing I wish for—all I'm really interested in is getting to know people (and animals and plants): I wish I could hear you say that you forgive me, if I've given you the impression that these words, and any others that may follow, mean anything more than just what they say, and I also, even more, wish I could hear you say that all this makes no sense to you, and passes your understanding, because it passes mine, and if both these things are so, we can share another image together (watch now while it comes and goes!), of us coming back on horseback, from riding through hill country we know well, alighting at sunset before our house that's gone quiet and dark, and whatever we find there, inside (I don't know), you'll put your arm on my shoulder and say, that's okay, what ever, whatever, that's okay. We'll go inside then, and while we're lighting the glass lantern, I'll know I can be Silent, the poet, helping to make songs for our voices, with power (just enough) to order words (and no order should last long), picked and passed on, from the box the milk-girl gave us, to songs that know nothing, that make no sense (what does?), that make us free, like fools.

Going home now, back from the West, by way of the North, walking a good step, not so slow as to keep me on the road much longer, but not so fast as to outrace the sun: I want to come home in twilight.

Going home, my gaze fixed ahead of me, not having to look behind to make sure all the plants and animals are following; I know. And this time I don't stop (as other times I might) to have a smoke with Stevie D, or drink some tea, or go to pick apples from some of my favorite trees, in orchards gone wild, where few people go. I didn't stop to peer in the windows of the ramshackle schoolhouse that was once a travelers' inn, in the days of the Colonies, and later a stop on the Underground Railroad, and a place where many a witch was burned in the talk of men (I've heard that the author of the *Dunwich Horror* learned some of his letters there); now it's full of old furniture and the webs of spiders past their spinning prime, and the back door's always unlocked, in case one of the mad walkers needs shelter from rain, and a dry box spring.

Feet kicking up leaves, walking by reaches and mazes of stone walls, piled there (who knows when?) to be boundaries, given meaning, and now allowed to be no more than what they are, stone walls, weed-covered. I didn't stop till I reached the crossroads and the sign, and the wayside chapel which I entered. It may not be what you think it is, but that's okay; we built it ourselves out of field stone, on the very spot where it's told that the most adept witch in the county used to make love with her brother (in the shape of a rampant bull) most every Sunday morning, in full view of the goodmen and their families of the Mountain, on their way to worship in the Hollow. They say the grass never grew there since. (And won't for a while more, at least, now there's a chapel there, built for travelers, and built to keep those memories imprisoned under stone and dancing feet.) (I eat breakfast there sometimes.)

I went in and sat a while. There was a candle burning in the circle of salt, and inside the circle, too, a piece of paper. At the top of the paper was a picture of me, stuck there with a safety pin, and an ink drawing of a piece of burnt toast, hovering over some leafless trees. There was a poem written below, in a girl's hand, and this is what it said:

> *Snake preserve you when you're distant*
> *come back quickly if you can,*
> *we will never be more different*
> *than we were when we began.*

I took off my goat-horn and laid it down near the poem, but far enough away so that some other pilgrim who might need it wouldn't feel afraid to take it. (And this all works out, I can tell you; the horn is gone now, and if you sit some other place near here, or far away, you never know, you may hear the horn blow, or whoever wears—or wore—the horn may come and tell you his story; I've heard of stranger things.)

Across the way I thought I heard the sound of people playing ball, and I wondered (it's true) how it would be to see them. So I thought I'd go greet the chickens first, although their day was done; leftward I turned, across the near yard, and down to the lower side of the barn, walking like an old fox on a frozen lake. (This scene is called "Before Completion.") There was King Something, and Rosemary, the goat, sleeping right on the oats.

The chickens were bedded down, side by side and heads to the wall; Tidewater, the rooster, lost among them, and the nameless chicks silent under the heat lamp, and three eggs I put in my pockets. Then sat on the bucket and took out my harmonica. At the first note all the hens squawked and looked around, and then went back to sleeping, when they recognized the tune. An old favorite, "I Gave My Love a Cherry," and then another, "Cluck Old Hen." And I made up a new one, after those, an evening, autumn, devotional, chicken-house raga.

Slowly, when I'd finished, the music made its way out into the dark, and not much more time passed before I followed, through the gate of the yard and uphill, past the yellowed peas and sweet peas, the late-blooming cosmos, the grape arbor: I want to tell you how I felt (although it's fairly clear already): quiet, and waiting, like a breath about to be breathed by someone else; alive, yet prior to saying so; walking, even by night, under a sun that never quite reaches noon, for then it would have to decline; feeling that I'd find things more or less the same; time never takes things too far away—

I knelt on the stone bench and looked in the window: I could see that the bowls, the food gone from in them, were stacked on the supper table, and people were sitting in the glow of the lantern at the other end of the room. There was my mother, and sister, and Kathy (Lila would be at Spirit Lake), and all the others, no one new, and my father gone forever, his cap and jacket hung on antlers near where he used to sit, his boots beneath them. And up on the stage, sitting on a milking stool, was old Haroon himself, frailer than I'd remembered him to be. His lips were moving, and the eyes of my people were intent upon him, sincerely, but I'd swear no sounds, or few, came from his throat. Still, he'd become no less articulate: the grotesque walking stick he carried whirled in his hands as if by its own power, and his hands and face assumed (and often held) expressions and combinations of expressions that stirred within me, like a wind in the rushes, memories I couldn't quite identify as mine, that I felt terrified to explore, though I didn't know why. And still, like all the others, raptly I watched him till he fell quiet. And just this more: somehow I know, though I can't say why, that he was telling about something very much like this, peering through a window and not being able to turn away, though what he saw moved him in ways unfamiliar and fearful.

And perhaps like me, and like old Haroon, you too are crouched as if outside a window, inhabiting darkness yet contemplating figures whose gestures, just now, have been favored with light (no more, just now, than the frail glow of the lantern someone lit and carried to the center of the room). But do not think your separation real, because it's not.

Perhaps you know now not to strain too hard to understand the last words of Haroon; we'll all know more about them some other time; the spaces will fill a little, no need to try. What eludes us is what always will, is all that's left out of this story (home so soon!), things we've forgotten, things we can't name or know nothing about, things we might have talked of, but now no matter, forms glimpsed from the corners of our eyes, burnt toast, shadows that walk behind us in the woods, and auras, the splendid and simple auras that are blooming round our heads.

Now Haroon had gone, away to sleep in some other room, I thought. And fewer people moved in the house. The light in the kitchen went out.

I entered and stood by the door for a moment, breathing in the loved smell, the best smell, of wood burning in the stove. Then I crossed to the Green Room, through the kitchen. There was a beam of warm light from under the door: low light, meant for my feet.

Inside the Green Room, we greeted each other in ways I don't need to tell, exactly; you must know how it feels, embracing good friends after some great sadness has come down, one you've not spoken about yet, but absorbed in the way you know best for you, surrendering a little here and there, but not completely till friends are around you—I will pass over what we did and said.

After a long time Raymond got up and poked around in the stove.

"Silent, we were all waiting for something tonight," he said, "it must have been for you."

I rubbed my chin. It must have been.

He went on:

"There was something about the sky tonight."

We all looked out at the sky, bright stars in air cold and clear, full October moon, all very close to the earth. There was something about it.

Dale went to put up some tea, and Verandah asked me about the toast. I knew she would.

I wanted to tell, but I couldn't begin. So I smiled. It would have to wait.

She and Raymond left the room.

"We're going to go tell Kamoo that you've come back," he said. I could hear them in the other end of the house, gathering the dogs for the walk down to the Hollow.

There was one thing I still wanted to know, so I turned to Uncle John and asked him,

"How did my father die?"

He seemed to want to hesitate a little.

"Sit down, son," he said.

"I am sitting down," I told him. (I was.)

I looked in his eyes, and he didn't look away. He took his bandana off his head and blew his great nose in it, and then he told me how my father had died. He didn't leave anything out.

While he was speaking Dale came in with some juniper berry tea, smelling like vegetable tears, warm down to my stomach.

When Uncle John finished we hugged and nothing more was said; I sat still, and couldn't sit still, and left him, climbed to my room, lit the small lantern, and held it up to the picture on the wall.

The picture on the wall was the last of my father's few paintings; he'd given it to me.

This is what it showed:

Night-time. A tiny walled town in the middle of a desert. Some dark green grass just outside the walls. A door shaped like a tombstone, and four striped domes that rise from behind the walls, a red one, a yellow one, a blue, and a green one. The sky full of stars that could be snowflakes, and a great golden lion lying outside the door, keeping watch. You can tell that no stranger comes or goes through without dealing with him. My father made the mane, and the nub at the end of the lion's tail, out of bits of twine he crumbled in his fingers, and mixed with the ochre paint. I was standing behind him when he did it.

"That looks really good," I told him.

"It's for you," he said.

The second picture on the wall wasn't there yet. Holding the lantern still, I put it right there myself, as best I could with just my eyes. But it's still there; I see it every time I come into the room, and there it stays when I've gone away, like an ikon in the chapel, protected by an increasing shroud of the best incense I may gather as I go: piñon from the Southwest, copal from Mexican market squares, the amber African myrrh, and sandalwood out of the East, and decked with silver and aluminum charms, little tin hearts and hands and feet and heads, strung on cotton threads, and hung with photographs of friends and ghosts and seacoasts, and paintings of fish and trees and weathered buildings, ceremonial poems on his birthday and the day he married and the day in October, ikon the more treasured because there's only one, and because my father is dead.

This is what it shows:

I've ridden the train away. They come back from

the Hollow without me. My father's happy as he can be. The four musicians decide to stay a little longer, and they, and the guests all camping on the orchard hill, and the people who live on the farm make music and dance. It's one of the best parties that anyone can remember, and the memories of some of the elders run very deep. My father's feet just can't stop dancing, in the shining leather boots, and some of the old men and women who haven't danced in years get up and try some steps, straining to sing, in animal voices, sounds we'll never hear again. Toward the end the musicians dress in fine old rock-and-roll costumes; I always smile to see them. They play one of the old songs my father loves, and he dances as high as he can. The hat nearly flies off his head, and the boots make sparks when they touch ground. He whirls around the campfire stumps. Sometimes he lightly touches my mother's hips. And then in the air, in the middle of a leap he dies. He dies. Beside the fire. The musicians are playing,

> *Lookin' for a job in the city*
> *Workin' for the man every night and day*
> *But I never lost a minute o' sleepin'*
> *Worryin' 'bout the way things might have been.*

Sunrise again. Someone's sitting on my bed to awake me. Kamoo. I've been asleep.

"Come on downstairs, Silent. Everyone's here."

So I roll over. I don't ask who. Feeling the goodness of waking in my own bed. Then up, with my head through the window. The morning sun, the same autumn, a little colder. Smell of some frost not yet gone from the grass. And the animals already awake. Luis chopping wood, his big loose sweater. Verandah gathering honeycomb, and Bob Paine himself wheeling in a barrow full of corn. We're going to have a feast. My sister down by the totems. She looks up and waves, and I wave too.

Walking out of the room, I pause and salute the two pictures for the first time. All action derives from this.

Down in the Big Room, everyone's there; it's true. All of the families from Spirit Lake have come, looking round the room in surprise (not much different from theirs!); some words fly back and forth, but all in fun; there's no more feud, perhaps there never was. And people from the Baby Farm were there, and from the farms our friends have, not far off in the Hardwood. And men from the town who'd heard the news, and all of you, were there. Every person I could think of was there, squeezed in whatever space there was for sitting, all there to hear the story—

One person, only, I missed. Where was old Haroon?

Marty spoke up. He'd followed Haroon's footprints far across the meadow: where they disappeared into the woods, a swath of leaves that seemed all glowing, and a smell of water somewhere ahead.

"I know the place," he said. "I'll show you some day."

Kamoo had a few first words to say:

"Silent's come home, friends. This part of his quest is over. He's found words and gone to the source of their power, and it's all inside him now, and he's learned as much as he yet can about burnt toast; it'll never manifest itself completely, for then its power would have to decline. But it all works out: now Silent can tell his story, and we'll all be able to see beyond the false dualities that kept us apart. The Two are One. We're all One, and always were. This old house is a ferry, and now we're casting off."

Kamoo knew just what had to be said. He made things clearer to us all, and some of the people in the room couldn't help singing.

Kamoo wanted to say something more:

"All this was meant to be; it's all part of the structure. Silent's been carrying the truth around in his pocket, since he awoke on the first day of this story. I rest my case."

I hadn't a clue what he was referring to, so I searched my overalls to bring it to light: not my harmonica, although it is said, and rightly so, that music is the means to the attainment of man's supreme goal; not the eggs, come from the chickens, though I was nearly ready to declare so—just one more pocket, a lump in the bottom, what my sister had given me when I passed her on the stairs so long ago:

I held it up; it dangled on its thread, and the audience breathed a breath: a jewel like an eight-pointed star, that seemed to hang still and yet to shimmer, like a pool of clear water stirred by a force not perceptible to the senses. The crest-jewel of discrimination, to be worn on the foreheads of fools, who see only one thing where there appear to be many. I held it close to my eyes and flecks of lantern light danced round the room; every brow seemed to wear the jewel. I held it closer still and it was true; from different corners Lila and Kathy merged into one; we all were one.

I touched the jewel to my forehead, and there it stayed; I haven't seen it since.

It was time to tell the story; the day was moving on in its own time, and I just a part of it, lost in it. I sat on the stool near the word-box, on the stage where the old Montgomery-Ward stove used to be, and looked at the beautiful faces in the room; we all looked around and smiled into each other's eyes ("Look in the eye," Ray says, " 'cause the eye don't lie"); I felt a rush begin, of what would soon be laughter. Someone from Spirit Lake stepped forth and unwrapped a silken parcel; inside was a large book of fine white paper, unwritten on, as old as the oldest tree in the Hardwood. Someone should write the story down.

Pete spoke up.

"I'd like to do it," he said.

He took the book onto his lap and opened his pen, and put on a fine italic nib, dipped into the green ink and squeezed. I heard the ink rush into the soft chamber.

"I'll speak slowly," I told him. "We have time."

He nodded his head. Time's what we have most of.

Then I closed my eyes, and thought of the spot on my forehead, until I didn't have to think of it any more. Slowly as if from one smiling voice a hum arose in the room and gathered strength as it discovered walls and ceiling—the best hum, the nameless one; I felt my back begin to move in a slow circle, as if wind and fire rode in intermingled spirals down my spine, and joined at the very bottom and climbed up again as sound, gathering form as it rose, pausing to touch and caress the centers of my body, navel, heart, throat, and head, till it knew all there was to tell, taking in all the power that lives in the silence, nearly becoming music as it reached my mouth—I worship and am the Sound that all sounds are born from—I could no longer hear the hum; I took a breath, a deep and long one, as deep as the drink a tree takes, sending sap to all its fruit, as long as this whole story, as long as my life till then and now, and longer; I smelled the wood-fire burning, and the harvest corn and the bread in the kitchen stove; I opened my eyes and saw the faces turned to me, lost myself in the faces, saw Peter, holding the pen above the page, waiting for the story to begin.

There's a very short and simple epilogue to this story (there may as well be); it takes place just a few days after the rest.

It's sunset, and King Something's jumped the fence, and gone down to visit the horses at Stevie D's. I put on my father's lumberjack shirt—the nights are colder now—and my wool cap, and go over the Mountain.

I find what I expect. He can't jump the stable fence, so he has to be content to smell the other horses, then turn around and let the other horses have a smell of him. I sit a while on the fence, and then lead him home. He doesn't mind.

It's a beautiful night; there's been some rain, and we're hiking up a stream bed that's become a little torrent, but the rain is gone; it's a clear night full of stars, and a few birds have lingered in the North: we hear them sing. We're walking in time, and sending splashes into the brush that catch the moon. I feel— it's as real as anything can be—the presence of my father, riding my shoulder like a bird, filling me with peace, but riding there, too, because it's peaceful. I can't say for sure that the crickets' song is not his heartbeat.

I give King Something plenty of oats and fresh water in his stall, and stand a while longer with him. When I go in the house at first there's no one to see. But in the Green Room, in the West end of the house, Raymond is standing by the stove, warming his hands, and Dale is on the sofa where the light's best, embroidering a sampler that says, "It's fun to make love." There's a little piece of peach pie left for me.

The three of us sit and stand there in silence while, soon, from out of the west, a sound we haven't heard for months comes over the fields: the first night wind of winter. It comes past the garden and seems to lean against the house; the walls sigh and tremble but don't give way; the three of us stand close together, like chambers of a heart beating inside a strong chest; we stand and listen to the wind that's come from so far, carrying his father on his back, wind and the father wind that pound on our door for food; the three of us look at each other as the wind passes by—not now at least, not yet; not this night but some other,

we'll know when
to let him in.

A Note on the Design of This Book

The text of this book was set by Fototronic CRT
in a type face known as Garamond. Its
design is based on letterforms
originally created by Claude Garamond, 1510–1561.
Garamond was a pupil of Geoffrey Troy and
may have patterned his letterforms on Venetian
models. To this day, the type face that
bears his name is one of the most attractive
used in book composition, and the intervening
years have caused it to lose little of its
freshness or beauty.

Composed, printed, and bound by The Colonial Press Inc.,
Clinton, Massachusetts
Typography by Elton Robinson

Line drawings by the author
Photograph on front cover by Barbara P. Fishman
Photograph on back cover by Peter Simon
Cover design by R. D. Scudellari